OTHER FIVE STAR WESTERNS BY WAYNE D. OVERHOLSER:

Nugget City (1997)
Riders of the Sundowns (1997)
Chumley's Gold (1999)
The Outlaws (2000)
Gateway House (2001)
Rainbow Rider (2001)
Wheels Roll West (2002)
Wild Horse River (2003)
The Law at Miles City (2004)
Twin Rocks (2005)
Bitter Wind (2006)
Sunset Trail (2007)
The Durango Stage (2008)
Pass Creek Valley (2009)
Shadow on the Land (2009)

LAW AT ANGEL'S LANDING

A WESTERN STORY

WAYNE D. OVERHOLSER

FIVE STAR
A part of Gale, Cengage Learning

GALE
CENGAGE Learning

Detroit • New York • San Francisco • New Haven, Conn • Waterville, Maine • London

LIBRARY OF CONGRESS CATALOGING-IN-PUBLICATION DATA

Overholser, Wayne D., 1906–1996.
  Law at Angel's Landing : a western story / by Wayne D. Over-
holser. — 1st ed.
    p. cm. — (Five Star Western)
  ISBN-13: 978-1-59414-907-8 (hardcover)
  ISBN-10: 1-59414-907-0 (hardcover)
  I. Title.
PS3529.V33L39 2010
813'.54—dc22   2010008448

First Edition. First Printing: July 2010.
Published in 2010 in conjunction with Golden West Literary Agency.

Printed in the United States of America
1 2 3 4 5 6 7 14 13 12 11 10

LAW AT ANGEL'S LANDING

CHAPTER ONE

I was in Yager's Bar along with the other town fathers of Angel's Landing when I heard the news that changed my life. In fact, it changed the lives of everyone who lived in Angel's Landing, and in all of Bremer County for that matter.

I included myself among the town fathers because I owned the only livery stable in town and was sheriff of the county, though I was younger than the others by more than twenty years, maybe too young to be called a town father.

Anyhow, I was standing at the bar along with Rip Yager, who owned the place, Kirk Bailey, who ran the Mercantile, Doc Jenner, and Joe Steele, the owner of the hotel. Outside of the county officials who came from the west end of the county, we were about the only ones in town who owned as much as the shirts on our backs.

At one time Angel's Landing had been a rip-roaring mining camp with as many as 5,000 people. That was when the strike above town on Banjo Creek brought men from all over the San Juans to Angel's Landing. I don't know who gave the camp its name, but it must have been some prospector from California where that kind of name was common. It sure didn't fit in Colorado where there weren't any boat landings and certainly no angels, but we were stuck with the name and we accepted it.

I'm Mark Girard. I'd lived in the county for eighteen years. My folks were among the first to arrive from Durango when the road was no more than a goat trail. It took a brave woman to make the trip on horseback, but my mother was a brave woman. She had to be to have followed my father all over the Colorado Rockies the way she had, but I never heard her complain.

I'd better qualify that last statement. I never heard her complain until after the mines petered out and my father wanted to move on. He was like most of the men in the mining country, always figuring he'd make it big the next time there was a gold strike. The majority never even made good wages and my father was part of that majority. This time my mother put her foot down.

"I've gone with you whenever and wherever you wanted," she said to my father, "risking my life and Mark's life just because you thought you'd get rich the next time somebody yelled he'd struck gold. You haven't and I don't believe you ever will. This time we're staying here. We've got a comfortable house. I've got a garden, a cow, and a flock of chickens. This is our home."

My father looked at her as if she'd gone daft. "There's nothing here no more, Martha. There never was much, just a pocket of gold up yonder on the creek that played out a month ago. In a few more weeks Angel's Landing will be a ghost town."

"Then we'll be ghosts," she shot back at him. "It's not fair to me to keep chasing the end of the rainbow and it's not fair to Mark, changing schools or winding up where there isn't any school at all." She shook her head. "I ain't holding you, Tom. Go anywhere you want to, but we're staying."

I was sitting in the kitchen and I remember the argument well, mostly because my parents had seldom argued about anything. My father had always called the shots and my mother had accepted any decision he made, but a mild woman can be stubborn when she has been pushed far enough and this time my mother had been pushed to that point.

My father couldn't believe he'd heard right. He yelled and stormed around for an hour, saying that a big strike had been made on the Dolores River above Rico, and he wasn't missing out on it. My mother simply turned her back and quit talking. My father got red in the face and was breathing so hard I thought he'd fall over in a fit, but he didn't. Finally he gave up and stomped out of the house. He saddled his horse and rode away, and that was the last we heard of him until a short time before his death.

I was scared when all the shouting had been going on. After my father left, I began to cry. When my mother turned to me, I saw that she had been crying, too. That stopped me. I'd seen my mother too tired to stand up, sick almost to death, and so hungry she was physically weak, but I had never seen her cry before.

I got up and went to her and said: "We'll make out, Ma. I'll get a job."

She put her arms around me and hugged and kissed me. "Of course we'll make out, Mark. We haven't starved before and we're not going to now."

Within a month Angel's Landing was close to being a ghost town just as my father had said. I remember walking along Main Street with its few brick structures and the long, double line of false-fronted frame buildings. Almost every one was vacant.

Just a few weeks before all of them had been occupied: stores, banks, offices, and a lot of saloons, gambling places, and whorehouses. Horses, buggies, freight wagons, and stagecoaches had filled the street until the traffic was so thick that it was hard to get to the other side. After the exodus I was lucky if I saw a cowboy's horse or Doc Jenner's buggy at one of the hitch rails.

I tried to get a job but there wasn't work for a man, let alone a ten-year-old boy. We might have starved when winter came and our garden stuff gave out if my mother hadn't been given the teacher's job. We didn't have more than five kids in school any time when I attended. The pay wasn't much, but it was enough to buy groceries to go along with the eggs and milk we had.

Through all those years Angel's Landing didn't have more than a hundred people and those people didn't change much. Doc Jenner had been there from the first and he stayed because he said he liked the country. He traveled all over Bremer County either in his buggy, if he was going downstream to one of the ranches, or on a horse if he had to go back into the mountains to look after some prospector who had broken a leg or had an accident with powder.

Rip Yager had a saloon in the early days and he stayed because there wasn't any competition and he could live cheap. "A man needs less money here," he'd say. "No place to spend it except over my bar or in Kirk's Mercantile."

Kirk Bailey stayed for pretty much the same reason. "There ain't many people around here," he'd admit, "but the ones who are here have to eat and I've got eating stuff to sell 'em."

I never told him, but the truth was he didn't have much to sell that we could eat. He didn't have anything else to speak of, either, just a few tools, powder for prospectors, clothes, guns, and tobacco. When Ma had to have cloth to make a dress for herself or a shirt for me, she went to Durango if she could combine it with seeing a dentist or going to a bank.

A stage brought the mail in twice a week. Sometimes she'd send an order with the stage driver, but, if she had to go, she'd rent a buggy from old Abe Riggs who ran the livery stable in those days. I always went with her until I was old enough to work regular because the road wasn't much better than it had been the first time we came over it.

When I was twelve years old, I got a summer job on a ranch about ten miles downstream from Angel's Landing. At first I was just a chore boy, but the boss liked me and I sort of grew into being a cowboy so it wasn't long until I had a full-time job. Ma had taught me all she could, but she kept after me to read and would order a book whenever she heard of one she thought I'd like.

We didn't hear a word from my father and after a while we gave up hoping. My mother never talked much about him, but one time at Christmas, when I guess we both were missing him more than usual, she said: "He's got too much pride to come back until he makes his strike and the chances are he never will."

The other kids grew up and left Angel's Landing because there wasn't any future for them there. I guess there wasn't much future for me, either, but I knew my mother would never leave, so I stayed with my job, going home every weekend and at Christmas. I was satisfied, maybe not being very ambitious and not craving excitement the way most boys did.

Besides, when my mother got too stove-up with rheumatism to teach, a young woman from Durango named Abbie Trevor came to town and took the school. I was the only young man around and she was the only young woman, so we just gravitated toward each other. I never figured I was in love with her or she was in love with me, but she was comfortable to be with and I figured that someday we'd get married, though we never talked much about it.

My father showed up late one spring three days after we got a letter saying that he was coming. It was just before my mother died. She'd been failing pretty fast. She told me one day that she wished she knew what had happened to my father before she died. I tried to tell her she wasn't going to die, but she knew better. She was pleased to get the letter, which was the first we'd heard from him since he'd left, and it gave her a new lease on life.

I met the stage that my father came on. He was older than

his years and more twisted up with rheumatism than my mother was. I guess I'd hated him for going off and leaving us, but I didn't hate him when I shook hands with him. It was too late to hate him. It was plain enough that he'd come back to die.

He walked home with me, moving very slowly as if each step hurt him. He hadn't said much when he got off the stage, just that he wouldn't have known me if I hadn't told him who I was. That wasn't to be wondered at, seeing as I was ten years old when he left Angel's Landing and I was twenty-eight when he returned. I had no trouble recognizing him, though he was only the shell of the man I remembered.

My mother had either been in bed or in her rocking chair for the past month, but the day my father got back she was up, wearing her best silk dress and having dinner on the stove. If it had been me, I think I'd have slammed the door in his face, but she didn't.

She stood on the porch, waiting for him to come up the walk. When he stepped beside her, she remained for a long moment, looking up at him, then she said—"Welcome home, Tom."—and hugged and kissed him. She cried a little and he cried, and I went back to the woodshed and worked with the bucksaw for a while.

It was a strange thing and I never pretended to understand how or why these things happen, but it was almost as if my mother had clung to life just long enough to see my father. The day after he got home she went to bed and a week later she was dead.

I had given up my ranch work and was living in Angel's Landing, having been elected sheriff a few months before. Since the county and town were peaceful enough, I didn't have much to do and I was able to stay home most of the time and look after my father. I knew this wouldn't last because there would be times when I'd be busy, but for the moment I was free to take care of him.

He was almost helpless, spending his waking hours in a big leather chair in the front room near the window where he could look out into the street that ran in front of our house. He could take care of himself as far as dressing and eating and tending to his bodily functions went, but that was all. I knew and I'm sure he knew that one day soon he'd simply give up and die.

He didn't say much. He just sat and stared into the street, maybe thinking about the old days when Angel's Landing had been a boom town. One day he thanked me for looking after him and I could see he wanted to talk, so I pulled up a chair and filled and lighted my pipe.

"I knew before I left Montana that if I didn't get here when I did," he said, "I'd never make it. Of course I didn't know whether your ma was still alive or not. I wouldn't have blamed her or you if you'd said you never saw me before in your life. It sure as hell was what I deserved."

I kept my mouth shut because that was what I thought. I just sat there and puffed on my pipe and waited to hear what else he had to say.

"Looking for gold gets hold of a man just like poker or whiskey does," he went on, "and with the wisdom of hindsight, I knew your ma was right. We all would have been better off if I'd taken a job somewhere and made a home for you and her. I kept thinking I'd make a strike and I could buy her all the things I dreamed about, but the truth was she never wanted them and I was too short-sighted to give her the one thing she wanted, a home."

He was short of breath. He stopped and puffed for a while, then said: "It takes a fool to chase the pot of gold at the end of the rainbow. Sometimes even when you know where it is, it still slips out of your fingers. That happened to me more'n once. When I did make my strike, I was too damned old and tired to work my claim, so I sold out and it was the other fellow who got rich off of it." He jerked a thumb toward the bedroom. "Go fetch my valise, will you?"

I brought it to him and laid it on his lap. He opened it and took out a tin box. He handed it to me, saying: "It's yours, boy. You deserve it and then some, looking after your ma and staying here like you done. I don't figure most sons would have done that. This was the only home she'd had since she was a girl, and I knew how much she thought of it. Only thing is I wish she had lived so the money could have done her some good."

I opened the box and looked at the biggest pile of greenbacks I ever saw in my life. Some were old and wadded up, and some looked as if they'd just been run off the press. They were of all denominations, but mostly big ones. I guess I stopped breathing for a while, thinking of all the things I could do with that money. When I looked up to thank him, I saw it was too late. He really had stopped breathing, his head tipped forward on his chest.

Like I said, I don't pretend to understand these things, but once he gave me the money, his heart quit beating. I don't know why, and I didn't know how or when he'd made his strike. Maybe it was just as well he died when he did; maybe he'd never made a strike at all.

CHAPTER TWO

I counted the money and found that there was more than $10,000 in the tin box. If my father had not made a strike, where did he get that much money? If, on the other hand, he had made the strike he said he had, why were some of the greenbacks wadded up, looking as if he had carried them in his pocket for fifteen years, and other greenbacks as new-appearing as if he had just run them off the press?

I will admit I had a vague notion that maybe he'd held up a bank or a train or a stage. There had been a lot of hold-ups in recent years, with Butch Cassidy and some of his friends being very active, but the Wild Bunch wasn't likely to include a man as old and bunged-up as my father must have been for several years.

Finally I quit stewing about it and accepted the fact that suddenly I had become a rich man, and I didn't have to account to anyone about where I got the money. The evening after my father was buried I walked to the teacherage, a one-room cabin back of the schoolhouse that was less than a block from my house. I asked Abbie Trevor to come to my place, that I had something to show her.

She hesitated, as if wondering what I could possibly have in my house that would interest her. She finally nodded and walked back with me. She was a tall woman, almost as tall as I was. Not exactly pretty, but certainly attractive, or she was to me at least. I think this quality stemmed more from her personality

15

than her good figure or perfect features, which in my judgment she didn't have.

Abbie made her own clothes. She had got along very well with my mother and had often spent a day at our house when school wasn't in session and had my mother help her with the dresses she was making. She had black hair and very dark brown eyes, the kind of coloring that set her apart from drab, run-of-the-mill women, and I'm sure this helped create my feeling that she was attractive. Along with this was the fact that Abbie read a good deal, and I often got into discussions with her that were thought-provoking and on subjects I would never talk about to Rip Yager or anyone else in Angel's Landing.

In many ways Abbie was like my mother and I had made up my mind that she was a woman I could spend the rest of my life with. I aimed to marry her and now I was a little nervous when I considered what I was about to do. Having been a bachelor as long as I had, I was reluctant to change my way of life.

I kept glancing at her, and then looking away. I must have irritated her because she asked tartly: "Have I got some dirt on the end of my nose?"

"Oh, no," I said, and then added: "I just like to look at you."

"Oh," she said, and gave me a questioning look as if I'd lost what good sense I'd been born with.

I had her sit at the kitchen table and then brought the tin box out from the bedroom. I set it on the table in front of her and said: "Open it."

She glanced at me again, still questioning what I was up to, I guess. She asked: "What is it, Pandora's box?"

"No," I said. "It's filled with good things."

She opened it and gasped, and then stared at the money as if she were frozen. Finally she shook her head and said: "I didn't think there was that much money in the world."

"Over ten thousand dollars," I said. "Maybe there are a few

more dollars somewhere in the world, but I don't figure there
are many."

"Ten thousand dollars," she murmured. "I haven't heard of
any bank being held up around here."

"I haven't, either," I said. "Do you know what I'm going to
do with it?"

"I don't have the slightest idea," she said, "but I would like to
know where you got it."

"Pa gave it to me. He told me he'd made a big strike in
Montana, but he was too old to work the claim, so somebody
else got rich off of it. Anyhow, he brought this much home, gave
it to me, and then died."

"It's incredible," she said, still sitting there as if frozen, her
eyes on the money. "Your mother used to talk to me about him.
She always said he was a proud man who would never come
back until he had made a strike, that he couldn't stand failure,
and would have to prove he had finally done what he set out to
do. I wondered about it when I first heard he was here. Did
your mother know about it?"

"I don't think so," I said, "though he spent some time alone
with her before she died, so he might have mentioned it. She
didn't say anything to me about it, and I think she would have
if she'd known."

"You've got to admire him for bringing the money," Abbie
said thoughtfully, "and not bragging about it and telling your
mother she had been wrong and hadn't had any faith in him.
He could have made her very uncomfortable."

I nodded. "He could have at that."

"Well, what are you going to do with it?"

"I'll go to Durango in the morning and put some of it in a
bank," I said. "I don't trust banks after what happened in
'Ninety-Three, but I don't like to leave it here in the house,
either. I thought I'd use some of it to buy the livery stable. I

sure don't get much salary from the county for being sheriff and it doesn't keep me busy, either. Then I thought we'd take a trip. Maybe go to California for a month or so."

"We?" She was shocked, then she got angry. "Will you tell me what you're talking about? You'd better get it through your head that I have no interest whatever in taking a trip with you."

I was sweating then. I didn't know how to say what I wanted to say, so I blurted: "I figured it would be our honeymoon. We don't have to go to California . . . we can go anywhere you want to. Niagara Falls maybe."

She stood up, and then she sat down. Her hands were trembling and her face started getting red. I had never seen her really furious before and I didn't know what I'd said or done that had brought this on.

"Just like that," she said in a low tone.

"Well, sure," I said. "Just like that. We've known each other for quite a while. We get along well. We enjoy being with each other. Leastwise I enjoy your company. It gets kind of lonesome living by myself."

"We get along well with each other," she said. "We enjoy being with each other."

She was sure bearing down hard on the word we. By that time I was sore. I thought I'd brought this up in the right and acceptable way, and she'd be pleased by what I'd said and be more than willing to marry me, but all I'd done was to make her as sore as a stepped-on bear with a sore toe.

"That's right," I said, "but maybe I was talking for myself."

"I suppose you get cold at night," she said sarcastically, "and that you get tired cooking for yourself and doing your own washing and ironing and everything else."

"Sure I do!" I shouted.

I aimed to say more, but I stopped, surprised that I had raised my voice to her. I never had before. Our relationship had been calm and serene and about as near perfect as it could have been, but now that I was finally asking her to be my wife, she was just plain mad.

Sure, I hadn't ever said it in so many words before, but I figured she understood how it was with me. Now I didn't know what to say, so I just sat and stared at her and didn't say anything.

Suddenly she wasn't angry. She asked breathlessly: "Mark, why haven't you asked me before?"

"I didn't want to get married as long as Ma was alive and depended on me," I answered, "especially after she quit teaching and you came to Angel's Landing. I didn't think it would be fair to you to ask you to live in Ma's house with me and her, and I couldn't very well leave her there at the last. Besides, I'd never been able to save much, and I didn't think that was fair, either. Not much happens in Bremer County, but, if something did, I'd have to handle it as long as I'm sheriff. I might get killed and leave you with a family to support and no money."

"I see." She sat staring down at her hands for a moment, then she rose. "I can't marry you, Mark. Not now."

She started toward the door. I jumped up and grabbed her by the shoulders and turned her around to face me. "Why?" I demanded. "I've got a right to know why. We've assumed for a long time that we'd get married someday. Now that Ma's gone and I've got this money and I can support you the way I want to, I don't see any sense in putting it off."

She shook her head and I swear she looked as if she really felt sorry for me. "Mark, if you don't know why I can't marry you, I certainly can't tell you."

I was so mad by that time I didn't care whether she knocked my head off or not, so I kissed her. I mean, I *really* kissed her. Oh, I'd kissed her before plenty of times, and we'd held hands, and I'd put my arm around her, but I guess I'd been backward, thinking that it wasn't the right time yet to let her know how I felt, but this time I did. I kissed her, long and hard, and I guess I must have held her so tightly that I came close to cracking one of her ribs.

When I finally let her go, she remained close to me for a moment, her lips inches from mine. She had returned my kiss. She had in no way discouraged me, and now she said in a low tone that was filled with regret: "You almost persuade me, Mark. Almost."

She turned away from me then and walked out of the house. All I could do was to stare at her back and consider the perversity of women, and wonder how in the hell could any man know how to handle one of them.

CHAPTER THREE

The next day I rode to Durango and deposited most of the money in a bank. When I returned, I used nearly all of the remaining cash to buy the livery stable, and then I hired an old man named Dutch Henry to stay in the stable and do as much of the work as he felt like doing.

Dutch Henry wasn't a Dutchman at all, but was an Irishman straight out of Cork or Killarney or wherever he came from. He got his name from a habit he had of saying: "It's an old Dutch proverb that chickens come home to roost." Or, if he got into a fight and was whipped, he'd say: "If I'd had my good old Dutch shillelagh, I'd have busted your skull open."

I'd known Henry ever since we'd moved to Angel's Landing. He was a prospector who'd been in and out of town and all over the San Juans from the day they'd made the first strike. He'd hit it lucky twice, made fortunes, and lost both of them.

Now he was an old man who was dead broke. He knew horses and physically he was still strong enough to do a day's work, so when I offered him a job for $5 a month plus his meals in the hotel and a place to sleep in the stable office, he jumped at it.

A dozen horses came with the business, but most of them were crow baits that weren't exactly assets to any livery stable, so I began trading them off and buying younger animals. We cleaned out the stable and I hauled most of the manure to my garden patch. The corrals were in bad shape, so Henry and I spent several days rebuilding them. Rip Yager wanted to know if

I expected another boom and I said a man never knew about the future.

I had just finished plowing the garden patch one afternoon when Abbie Trevor came over. I hadn't seen her to talk to since the evening I'd asked her to marry me and she'd walked out of the house.

I hadn't given up on her, but I sure wasn't aiming to run around after her, begging her to tell me why she couldn't marry me, so I'd decided to wait her out and let her make the next move. She did, which proved I was using the right tactic.

Abbie sauntered up to the garden fence and leaned on a post as if nothing had happened between us. She asked: "How are you, Mark?"

"Fine," I said. "How are you?"

"Fine," she said amiably. "You aiming to put a garden in this summer?"

"If I get around to it," I said.

"I guess it's late enough now so we won't have to worry about a frost."

"I wouldn't bank on it," I said. "I've seen it snow here on the Fourth of July."

"I know," she said, "but you can't wait any longer to plant the garden. Your mother used to say you were good at eating garden stuff, but not very good at planting and raising it."

"That's right," I said. "When I get down on my hands and knees and weed a row of carrots, I always pull more carrots than weeds."

"I'll make you a proposition," she said. "I'll put the garden in and do the weeding if you'll harrow the ground and do the ir-rigating. I'm not very good at that."

"Fair enough," I said. "I'll harrow it after supper. If I forget to turn the water on from the ditch when the garden needs it, remind me."

"I will," she said.

She started back toward her house, then stopped when I called: "Abbie, I just got a new red-wheeled buggy! How about taking a ride with me tomorrow afternoon?"

"I'd love to," she said.

So we were friends once more, I thought as I watched her walk back to her house, and I wondered if she expected me to ask her to marry me again. I probably would someday, but I was sure going to let her worry a while. She was pushing thirty, an old maid by almost any standard, so she was the one who ought to do the worrying.

I harrowed that evening after supper as I'd promised. The ground was just right for planting. It had rained a few days before and now the red soil had dried out enough so it could be worked but was moist enough to sprout the seeds.

The next morning Abbie was putting out the garden by the time the sun was up. When I came home at noon, she'd finished. I picked her up early in the afternoon. She had taken a bath and was all bright and shiny and clean-smelling.

"You're a regular workhorse when you get started," I said.

"Oh, Mark, it was so much fun," she said. "When I lived in Durango, I always had a garden and I've missed it since I came here. It isn't often that you catch the ground just the way it was this morning, so I kept at it until I finished."

I drove up Banjo Creek for no particular reason except that I hadn't been along it for a while. Old shacks and cabins lined the stream, most of them dating back to the boom days. Now only a few were still standing. During the winter the prospectors who didn't have a home anywhere else moved into the ones that were livable, but most of them were half-rotted piles of logs and boards. The parts that were usable, such as windows and doors, had been stolen a long time ago.

Just below the mouth of the cañon we passed what had been

the red-light district in the boom days, largely double rows of shacks on opposite sides of the creek. The one exception was a large frame building, two stories, that had been known as the Pleasure Palace.

The Palace had been run by a madam named Maggie Martin and had been a very successful business. The gossip ran that she'd operated a high-class place with pretty girls, a bar, and expensive furniture, and that she'd made more money than the miners had ever taken out of the gravel along Banjo Creek. I was only a kid when Maggie was going full blast, but I remember walking along the creek and seeing the girls drying their hair in the sun.

I knew, or maybe sensed, that there was something evil about the girls, but somewhere along the line I got acquainted with Maggie. She was a big, red-headed woman who was as friendly as a pup. She spotted me walking past her place, so one day she called: "Bud, come over here!"

One of the girls cried: "What are you up to, Maggie? He's just a boy."

Maggie snorted. "What do you think I'm up to? I'm just going to give him a piece of cake."

My first impulse had been to run, but my curiosity got the best of me. I liked cake and we seldom had any. Besides, Maggie didn't look dangerous, so I walked up the path to the porch where the girls were sitting. They all wore robes of one kind or another, but Maggie had the loudest—a red silk one that came down to her ankles.

When I stopped and looked up at her, she asked: "What's your name, bud?"

"Mark Girard."

"Well now, that's a fine name," she said. "Your daddy a miner?"

"Yes."

"Does he ever come here?"

"I don't know."

"Maggie!" The same girl who had spoken up before glared at her. "You keep this up and you'll get all of us into trouble."

Maggie whooped a big laugh and slapped her leg. "Naw. No man who has a fine boy like Mark here ever comes to the Pleasure Palace. Come on, Mark. We'll go to the kitchen and see if there's any cake left from supper last night."

I followed her down a long hall. I had a glimpse of the parlor with its big piano and fancy chairs with scroll backs and silk-covered seats and a couch covered by red velvet that was long enough to seat about six people. The kitchen wasn't any different from ours except that it was a lot bigger and had a Negro woman standing beside the big range, stirring something.

"You shouldn't bring that boy in here, Maggie," the Negro woman said.

"I ain't going to hurt him," Maggie said. "He's hungry like most boys."

She went back into the pantry and came out a moment later with a big slice of chocolate cake and a glass of milk. She had me sit down at the table and eat the cake and drink the milk. It struck me that whenever I looked up and saw her watching me, she seemed as hungry as I was, but I didn't know then what she hungered for.

After that Maggie asked me to come in whenever she saw me and always gave me cake or pie. After a while the girls and the Negro woman who had argued with her about asking me into the house quit fussing and sometimes even talked to me. Every time I left, Maggie would warn me about not telling my folks I'd been inside the Palace.

One day after the boom petered out, I walked past and saw that the place was empty. Maggie hadn't told me she was leaving. She'd just moved out, and she'd taken her girls with her. I went in and looked around. I felt funny and sad, standing there in the empty house that echoed every time I took a step.

I never went back inside. I just didn't feel like it. I'd liked Maggie and the Negro woman and the girls I'd talked to and I missed them. I often wondered what happened to them. I suppose they drifted on to Silverton or Rico or Ouray or any other camp that promised business.

Another thing I've always wondered about was what my mother would have said if I had told her about being in the Palace, but I'm glad I didn't. She would probably have gone to the marshal and complained about Maggie tying to corrupt her son.

Now, driving past the dilapidated building, the windows and doors all gone so that it looked like a toothless old man, I blurted out the story to Abbie.

When I finished, she looked at me curiously, maybe wondering if I'd told everything. She asked: "Just what was Maggie hungry for?"

I shrugged and wished I hadn't told her. I said: "Your guess is as good as mine."

Abbie sniffed. "The girl and the Negro cook were right. Maggie shouldn't have taken you inside."

My mother would have said the same thing. It struck me that the good women of the world would stick together and condemn Maggie, but I didn't see it that way. Sitting at her table and eating pie and cake were among the most pleasant memories of my childhood.

CHAPTER FOUR

Angel's Landing sat in the middle of a small valley below the jaws of Banjo Cañon. Here, just above the mouth of the cañon, the cliffs were so close that this particular spot was known as the Narrows. The stream that boiled through the opening was not more than three feet wide.

The road followed a shelf that was twenty feet above the water and was barely wide enough for one vehicle. Traffic had been nothing but trouble here during the boom days, but in spite of all the talk about blasting a wider road out of the side of the cañon, nothing had been done.

Abbie shut her eyes until we were out of the Narrows and had returned to the water level. She shook her head and tried to smile. She said: "I've been over that piece of road a dozen times since I came here to teach. I'm ashamed of myself, but I guess I'll always be afraid of it. I don't know how they managed when so many people lived up here in the cañon."

"They had trouble," I said.

The cañon floor widened ahead of us until it was about fifty yards across. The gravel had been panned and re-panned and panned again, and I suppose a man could still get some color here if he tried, but no one had worked the ground for years, and now brush and small cottonwoods had grown up until the bottom of the cañon was green with only a spot here and there showing the gray gravel that had been characteristic of the cañon during the mining days.

27

In the Narrows the towering walls cut out the sunlight, but above it where we were now the cliffs were far enough apart and slanted back from the bottom so that normally the sunlight touched practically the entire bottom. Abbie was the first to notice that suddenly there was no sunlight.

"Mark," she cried, "look at the sky! What's happening?"

I glanced up. "I guess we've got a storm coming in."

"But it's no common storm," she said. "Let's go back."

I didn't say anything, and I didn't turn back for a moment, but I'll admit I was scared. We had heard the rumbling of thunder for quite a while, and had seen flashes of lightning, but that was nothing out of the ordinary this time of year.

Usually from this point we could see snow-capped peaks north of us, and, if we found the exact spot, we could catch a glimpse of Engineer Mountain, but not today. Everything to the north was hidden by the clouds that were racing toward us and now had blotted out the sun.

I had seen storms that were ring-tailed wowsers. I had seen plenty of black clouds, and I'd heard thunder that had jarred the earth, but I had never seen a sky as forbidding as this, or thunder that sounded as if it was going to bring the cliffs down on top of us.

No one could adequately describe the sky. It was more than black; it held a weird, frightening shade of purple except where the lightning slashed across it and brought its own peculiar flickering light into the bottom of the cañon, which had become almost as dark as night.

"Turn around, Mark!" Abbie cried. "I'm scared. It looks like the end of the earth."

It did for a fact. I was shocked that the change had come so rapidly. The smell of rain was in the air. I could see it directly ahead of us, moving downstream like a curtain that had been pulled across the cañon.

This had happened in what must have been only a matter of seconds, although it seemed much longer. I would have turned back the first time Abbie asked me if I hadn't been curious about what was happening. In fact, I couldn't quite believe what I was seeing, but I believed it now, and I knew that, if we were caught in the cañon, we'd be climbing the sides or we'd drown.

I said—"Hang on."—and turned the rig around and applied the whip.

We went rocketing down the rough road as fast as the horse could run. He was boogered plenty and glad to go, sensing, I guess, that this was no place to linger. Abbie hung on, all right, her face a pasty green.

The thunder seemed to be one continuous roar, the echoes of the previous clap still pounding at our ears when the next one came, the lightning flashes snapping so fast that the cañon seemed to be alternately light and dark every other second.

A savage wind was slamming us from the rear and rocks were rolling down the sides of the cañon by the time we reached the Narrows. It would be a deathtrap unless we were just plain lucky. We were. We pounded through the Narrows like a bob-tailed meteor, with good-size rocks hitting the road in front of us and behind us and rolling into the cañon below us.

Abbie grabbed me by the arm and hung on as if somehow I was her hold on life. The rocks were big enough to smash our buggy and kill the horse if one had hit him on the head, but we made it through by the grace of God and not by my skilful driving.

Just as we roared out of the Narrows, the lightning struck a pine tree beside us. It was the closest I had ever been to lightning at the moment when it actually struck something. The blinding light burst out into a blossom of flame like an exploding shell.

29

I could smell the brimstone; for a moment I thought I was blinded. Abbie hid her face against my shoulder and began to cry. The horse reared and pawed at the air with his front hoofs, then decided that it was not the proper place to stop and meditate, so he started toward town as if the devil had tied a knot in his tail.

We were all right then. I knew it and I think Abbie knew it, but you don't get over a scare like that in a matter of seconds. As I pulled up in front of my house, I yelled: "Run for it! I'll put the horse away!"

The rain was coming down hard before I stopped. Abbie ran for the front door, but before she reached it, she was soaking wet. It didn't seem to be rain. The sky simply opened up and dumped the water so it was like being under a waterfall. Of course I was wet, too, before I got the horse unhooked and led him into the shed. When I lunged through the back door, Abbie was standing in the middle of the kitchen with water dripping off her and making a puddle on the floor.

She was the most bedraggled-looking woman I ever saw in my life. She said solemnly: "Mark, I'm drowned."

We laughed with more hysteria than humor. I took her into my arms and kissed her wet lips, then I shoved her toward the door of what had been my mother's bedroom and gave her a pat on the behind.

"You'll find towels in the top drawer of the bureau," I said, "and a robe in the closet that will fit you."

I went into my room and changed clothes. The rain was still pounding on the roof. There must have been hail in it because the racket sounded as if someone was up there banging away with a hammer. I figured I'd have a roof to fix when this was over. The shingles on the livery stable would probably be in splinters, too.

When I returned to the front room, Abbie was standing near

the door, wearing my mother's blue robe. It was pretty skimpy for Abbie and reached only to her knees, my mother having been several inches shorter than Abbie. Her hair was a mess. She gave me such a forlorn look that I laughed.

"Don't you dare," she threatened, and then giggled. "You still want to marry me after seeing me this way?"

"Yes, I want to marry you," I said.

"I guess this ought to be the supreme test," she said.

She came to me and kissed me. So it was settled, I thought, and was vaguely uneasy. I wondered why we had gone through all the messy business of her having to tell me she couldn't marry me, and, if I didn't know why, she couldn't tell me.

Nothing had been changed as far as I could see, but now for some reason she was willing. I was sure she wasn't wearing a thing under the robe, a thought that I found exciting, but at that particular moment I was in no mood to pursue the matter.

The storm had petered out to light rain and an occasional flash of lightning, but suddenly we heard a new sound, a terrifying roar that made the earth tremble. For an instant I thought it was another giant clap of thunder and immediately knew it wasn't, and then wondered if it was an earthquake.

We rushed to the front door and yanked it open. What we saw was more frightening than the sound had been. A ten-foot wall of water was pouring through the mouth of the cañon. I had never seen anything like it and I hope I never do again.

The flood swept out into the valley, the crest gradually disappearing. The backwater rushed toward us. I knew it would reach Main Street and my house and barn. The livery stable, too. Abbie was hanging onto me with both arms, sniffling and shaking and saying that she thought the danger was past.

"It is," I said. "This isn't going to hurt us."

But those words were for Abbie. I wasn't that sure. We couldn't do a thing but stand there and wait. The water was already around the house. I didn't think we could outrun it to higher ground, so we stood there and watched.

The shacks along the creek were gone, along with the old Pleasure Palace building, the weathered boards and beams bouncing on the water like corks as they floated past. The power of the flood was unbelievable. The water covered the valley from one side to the other, but our house and the business buildings on Main Street were on higher ground and I could see now that we were out of the main current and would not be hurt.

It was different closer to the banks of the creek where nothing stood against the power and violence of the stream. Pine and cottonwood trees had been torn out by the roots and were sweeping past us, turning and twisting as the whirling muddy water carried them downstream.

Abbie was quiet now. I held her in my arms and she was satisfied to stay there. She didn't move or say anything, but huddled against me as if finding comfort in my strength. We stood there a long time, until the water began to recede, leaving the ground around the house thoroughly soaked with puddles that would remain until the sun came out and sucked the water from the earth.

I picked Abbie up and carried her into my mother's bedroom. I put her down and covered her with a quilt. She had been shivering. The air had turned very cool and was heavy with moisture, but I wasn't sure whether she was cold or still frightened.

"I'll build a fire and put the coffee pot on the stove," I said.

"Get in here beside me, Mark," she begged. "Make me warm. I'm freezing."

I lay down beside her. She pulled the quilt over us and I put my arm around her so that her head was on my shoulder. She kissed me and said: "I'm glad I was with you, Mark. If I'd been alone, I'd have been in hysterics. All of the talk about the goodness of Mother Nature is crazy. She's a monster that tries to devour us."

"She did today," I agreed. "I hope I never see that side of her again."

"I want to be with you always," she said. "Don't ever let me go, Mark."

I held her shivering body close to mine until she was warm. When she fell asleep, I slipped out of the bed and shut the door. I crossed the front room and looked out on an ugly sea of mud. The water was slowly draining away from the valley land that it had flooded and would soon be contained inside the banks of the creek.

Piles of boards and uprooted trees dotted the valley. The crest of the flood was somewhere below us now, and I wondered what was happening to the ranchers who lived downstream from us and anyone who might have been on the road beside the creek.

Later I heard that no one was drowned, but a great deal of damage was done to buildings and hay meadows and roads before the high water poured into Las Animas River. All of us who lived in Angel's Landing felt lucky that the town wasn't swept away, which it would have been if the business block had been laid out closer to the creek, and lucky, too, because no lives were lost.

But we did lose something that was of great value to us—our way of life. We found that out a week later.

CHAPTER FIVE

Bremer County roads were never kept up very well because the county was small and lacked both money and equipment, but the road to Durango was the only avenue we had to the outside world. All of our mail and freight came in over it, so we had to get it open.

For the next five days after the flood every able-bodied man in Angel's Landing and all of our teams worked on the road below town, moving rocks and driftwood, scraping the road, and digging back into the bank where the water had cut away so much of the road that a rig couldn't get by.

We still didn't have a boulevard when we got done, but the road was passable as far as the county line. On the sixth day I rode to Durango and gave the commissioners hell for not cleaning up their end of the road. They promised to get work started on it immediately, and I made some threats about building a new road over the mountains to Silverton, an idle threat because those were mountains you just didn't go over. I knew it and I knew they knew it.

I'm sure I didn't scare the commissioners, but they assured me the road would be open within the week, and I guess it made me feel better to threaten them because they had always more or less ignored the road up Banjo Creek, and people in Angel's Landing had been sore about it as long as I could remember.

After that there wasn't much we could do but wait. We had

plenty of staples in the Mercantile, but Kirk Bailey never had much variety and he had less now. If the road wasn't opened in another week or so, we'd have to bring supplies in on a pack train.

The day after I'd been to Durango, we got together in Yager's Bar for a drink and some talk about what we'd do if the Durango people didn't keep their promise. That was when we heard the news that changed our lives.

The day was a hot one, and we were drinking beer that was a long way from being cold, Rip Yager's ice being long gone, when we heard someone yelling in the street.

"Sounds like that feller's getting murdered," Rip said. "Better go see about it, Mark."

I didn't figure anybody wanted to murder anybody else in Angel's Landing. We hadn't had any real trouble since I'd taken the star. My guess was that some cowboy from below town was getting worked up enough to raise a little hell, which was the worst that ever happened in Angel's Landing, so I set my beer down and went out through the batwings into the hot sunshine.

It wasn't a cowboy who was doing the yelling. It was old Catgut Dolan, a prospector we figured was older than Engineer Mountain. He'd been all over the San Juans a dozen times; he'd prospected up and down Banjo Creek so often he could draw a map of every rock in the cañon from memory, and he never had made a strike.

I guess he lived off fish he caught and animals he shot and berries he picked and maybe roots he dug up. Sometimes he'd work a few days, just long enough to buy salt and ammunition and clothes, then he'd head out again. He had a white beard and long hair. He stunk so badly nobody could stay in the same room with him, and that made him about as popular as a skunk with hydrophobia.

Catgut was standing beside his burro in the middle of the

street, waving his battered old hat and yelling something about striking gold. When he saw me, he pulled his gun and started shooting at the sky.

I walked up to him, figuring he was drunk. I said: "Cool off, Catgut. This is pretty early in the morning to be caterwauling like this."

He stopped yelling and shooting long enough to hear what I said. He stuck his gun back into his holster and jabbed a forefinger in my direction.

"I ain't had a drink in two weeks," he said. "You figger I'm just a dirty, no-good old prospector, don't you? You high and mighty town bastards figure I'll never amount to anything, don't you? Well, by God, I struck gold, and I can buy the whole bunch of you out."

Of course I didn't believe it. I said: "Go over to the jail and sleep it off, Catgut. I'll put your burro in the stable and take care of him till you're ready to start out again."

He ignored me. He went over to his burro and untied a partly filled sack and shook it at me. "Here it is, Sheriff. I've got more gold here in this sack than you ever saw. I found it right under your nose."

I took the sack from him, surprised at how heavy it was. All the time I was thinking that I'd have to shove him into jail by force, but mostly out of curiosity I opened the sack and took a look at the rocks that were in it. I wasn't an expert on such matters, never having had any desire to go prospecting, but I'd seen some high-grade ore and this looked like the real thing.

I wheeled around and headed for the saloon. Catgut took after me, yelling: "You can't have it! I'm going to Durango and file my claim. Give it back, damn it!"

I beat him through the batwings and emptied the sack on the bar. "Take a look," I said.

Catgut was yelling: "That's mine! You can't have my gold.

I'm taking it to Durango!"

Nobody paid any attention to him, but Bailey, Doc Jenner, and Joe Steele had lived in the mining country most of their lives, and they knew gold when they saw it. I didn't pay much attention to them, though. Rip Yager was the one I watched because he had done some prospecting and had made enough money out of one mine to buy the saloon.

They all nodded and looked at each other and nobody said a word for a good minute or more. I don't think they even breathed. At that moment I didn't hear a sound except the buzzing of a big fly on one of the windows. Rip Yager stood there as if frozen, staring at the gold, then Dutch Henry walked in.

Dutch was more of an expert even than Rip Yager. He asked: "What was this old goat yelling about?"

"I hit it!" Catgut screamed. "You didn't ever think I would. You're younger'n I am but you quit looking. I didn't, and I found the biggest damn' vein you ever saw right here under your nose."

Dutch picked up a chunk of the ore, looked at it, then looked at me. He started to say something, choked, and finally managed: "By God, boss, the old buzzard finally found something."

"Don't call me an old buzzard," Catgut fumed. "I'm a millionaire and you'd better start treating me like one. I'm gonna record my claim and then I'm gonna go to a bank and get the backing I need. I'm gonna run a tunnel into the side of the mountain and I'll take out more high-grade than you ever seen."

Dutch kept picking at the ore, shaking his head and breathing hard. He asked: "Where'd you get this, Catgut?"

"You think I'm gonna tell you before I get to Durango?" Catgut screamed. "I ain't as stupid as you think. You just foller back up Banjo Creek when I show up with wagons and machinery and powder, and you'll find out where I found it.

37

I'm fixing to call my mine the Lucky Cat."

He dropped his rocks back into the sack and stalked out of the saloon. Dutch Henry shook his head at me. "It's a kind of fever, boss. I figured I was over it, but I ain't. I'm quitting my job and I'm going up Banjo Creek. I'll stake me a claim right beside old Catgut's."

"You've been eating regular lately, Dutch," I said. "Take the day off and borrow a horse, and then come back to work tomorrow."

"Nope," Dutch said. "I'm quitting."

He stalked out of the saloon. We watched him go, everybody still too shocked to say anything until after the batwings slapped shut behind him. Then Rip picked up a bottle and five glasses and walked to a table, jerking his head at us to follow.

We sat down and Rip poured our drinks, then set the bottle on the table slowly and carefully. He said: "Gentlemen, I'm the oldest man here and I reckon I've seen more strikes and boom towns than any of you. I'm a 'Fifty-Niner. I came to Denver when there wasn't nothing but a few shacks on Cherry Creek. I just want to say one thing. I like living in Angel's Landing, but in a few days I ain't gonna like it one bit. It'll take Catgut a day or two to get to Durango. It'll just take another day or two after that for the parade to start."

Kirk Bailey and Doc Jenner were about ten years younger than Rip Yager, and Joe Steele was younger than they were by another ten years or more. They all looked at Rip and scowled, thinking, I guess, that they'd seen the elephant about as many times as he had, but nobody tried to argue with him.

"You're not much different than the rest of us, Rip," I said, figuring I could talk to him better than the others. "I was just a kid during the boom days here, but I remember how it was, a killing every day and a wide-open camp. I saw so many rigs and horses in the street that I had a hard time getting across to the other side. It'll be the same thing all over again."

"Not if I can help it," Rip said somberly.

"You can't help it," Doc Jenner said. "I've liked it this way, too. I reckon we all have. I've made a living and I haven't had to work very hard doing it. Now I'll be up twenty hours a day digging bullets out of men and sitting up with them that have the fever and doing my best to save some old floozy who's taken too much laudanum. Maybe I'll just leave town."

"No you won't," Bailey said. "You own too many town lots to go off and leave 'em. And me, I'm going to send a big order to Durango. I'll take it myself. It's still our town. Maybe we'll all get rich. Maybe not. Either way, we'll stay and ride it out."

I think all of us agreed to that, but we still didn't say anything for a long time. It was like sitting up with a corpse the day before the funeral, the corpse of someone we all loved. We knew what would happen, we knew we couldn't stop it, and we knew we'd stay in Angel's Landing. I don't think any of us doubted that, though Rip had some questions.

"We ain't incorporated," Rip said after a time. "You're all the law there is, Mark. When you ran for sheriff, you didn't contract to take on a job like this. You can resign and nobody will fault you for it."

"I'll hang and rattle," I said, a little sore that he'd think I'd quit. "I've got to hire some deputies and I'll need more money to do it."

"You'll have to see the commissioners," Rip said. "I don't know what they'll say, though, with two of 'em coming from the west end of the county and not giving a damn about what happens to Angel's Landing."

"And the third one a rancher who lives down the creek," Doc Jenner said. "He ain't gonna be much interested in spending more money, either."

"You're gonna need two or three deputies," Kirk Bailey said.

"If the county won't give you the money, we'll raise it privately. We've got to keep the lid on from the start."

"By God, that's right," Rip Yager said through clenched teeth, "and I aim to help do it."

I didn't know what he meant and I didn't ask, but it was plain that they all had their doubts about how well I could handle anything more dangerous than arresting drunks and throwing them into jail to sleep it off. So far that was all I'd had to do.

I never pretended to be fast with a gun or an alley fighter, and I knew damned well that these four men didn't think I was tough enough or mean enough to handle a boom town's problems. I wasn't sure, either, but I was sure I wasn't quitting.

CHAPTER SIX

The Bremer County Courthouse was a two-story, frame structure that needed a coat of paint and a new roof. It had been built the year of the boom, when nearly all of the people of the county lived in Angel's Landing or above it on Banjo Creek.

That situation had changed with the development of dry farming in the west end of the county, where at least three-fourths of the county's inhabitants now lived. The county seat would have been moved before this if there had been any town of consequence in the west end, but there were only a few scattered post offices and stores. Nothing more.

So, with the courthouse already built in Angel's Landing, no one pushed very hard to move the county seat even though it was a long and difficult trip for anyone in the west end to come to the county seat on business. I thought the distribution of the people also accounted for the rundown condition of the courthouse. None of the county officials except me gave a damn.

All of this was very much in my mind as I climbed the squeaking stairs to the commissioners' office. I was beaten before I started because I knew their attitude toward raising taxes or using county money for anything, even if it was available. They figured the best government was no government, that democracy would function without money if they refused to spend it.

I didn't see any way that Angel's Landing could solve the

problem of law enforcement unless we incorporated. That, too, meant more taxes, but, with the influx of people we were bound to have, we could afford it. We'd have to do it eventually, but it would take time that we didn't have.

Joe Loring and Frank Bohannon were the commissioners from the west end of the county. They were in Angel's Landing only a few days each year taking care of their public duties. Both were farmers, and, since that was their means of making a living, they spent most of their time at home.

The third commissioner, Paul Kerr, was a rancher who lived about five miles below town on Banjo Creek, and, although he was a little more sensitive to our needs than the other two, he was almost as tight-fisted as they were when it came to spending tax money.

I found Loring and Bohannon in their office, puffing away on their pipes, their feet cocked on their desks. They spoke to me in a guarded sort of way, as if figuring I was there for some reason that they would not approve of. They were dead right.

I didn't like them and they didn't like me, but it was not personal as much as it was a matter of attitude toward how the county government should function. I believed that paying taxes was not a bad thing if we, the people, got something for our money, but they held the notion that it was their business to see that no taxes were levied, therefore no tax money could be spent.

"Paul around?" I asked.

Loring shook his head. "He ain't been in the office all week."

"We won't be here after today," Bohannon said. "We're going home tomorrow and we won't be back till harvest is over."

"Well, you're a majority," I said. "It's a good thing I caught you today if you're leaving town. Something's happened that's going to turn our lives around."

"That so?" Loring said, as if unconcerned. "I can't think of anything that would turn my life around unless we get a dam and I'm able to irrigate my land."

"And that ain't gonna happen," Bohannon said.

I told them about Catgut Dolan's strike, adding: "I know how it was in the old days because I lived here. It wasn't safe for a woman to go down the street. They had a man for breakfast every morning. People were robbed right and left. We'll have it all over again."

"That ain't gonna turn my life around," Loring said complacently. "I'll stay home if it gets that bad. Paul can do what has to be done. Me 'n' Frank will do what we have to do by mail."

Bohannon nodded. "It's up to you to enforce the law." He grinned and winked at Loring. "It's what you get paid for, ain't it?"

I felt like slugging him. I was paid in pennies and he knew it. I'd never have opened my mouth if the situation had remained as it had been when I was elected, but a man deserves more than pennies when he has to risk his life doing his job. I held on to my temper, knowing it wouldn't do any good to blow up.

"I want to hire two deputies," I said, "and I want the county to pay their salaries."

"You've been feeding on locoweed," Loring said.

Bohannon put his feet on the floor and stood up. He said: "Mark, you know there ain't no fund we can use to pay them. You'll have to do the best you can by yourself."

I knew there wasn't any such fund, but I figured they could find the money if they wanted to. I stood there a moment, staring at them, knowing that this was what I'd hear and still being disappointed. I realized I'd had a slim hope they might at least listen.

"The next time you come to Angel's Landing," I said, "you'll know why I asked for deputies. I think you'll wish to hell you had provided a couple of them."

I wheeled and stomped out of the office, knowing that I had to get out before I told them what cheapskates I thought they were. I left the building and walked around to the back, where the jail was located.

The jail was a log building. The front half was one big room, which was my office; the rear held the cells, a large one I used for drunks, and two small ones barely large enough for a bunk and space for a man to stand up. These cells had no windows and no peepholes in the doors, so it must have been hell to have been locked up in one, especially during hot weather. I never had used them, although I'm sure they had been used before my time as sheriff.

I sat down at my desk and smoked a pipe, thinking the situation over. The more I thought, the more I came to one conclusion. I had to have at least one deputy to start with, and I had to have him before the boom hit Angel's Landing.

There was no county money, so I wound up with one answer that didn't suit me worth a damn. I'd pay him myself. Later, I'd hire more than one. That meant I'd have my own private army to enforce the law, which in turn meant I'd have the leverage to force other businesses to pay their share. Illegal, sure, but I figured I'd be justified in doing it, and I knew it had been done in other places in similar situations.

The first job was to find the right man. There wasn't any in Angel's Landing, so I'd have to go to Durango. I had one man in mind, but I wasn't sure I could persuade him to take the job. There was one other thing I intended to do, and that was to see Paul Kerr, the third commissioner.

I knew I'd hear the same story from Kerr that I'd heard from the others, but I had to try. When a man is standing in the path of an avalanche, he'll do anything he can, and I figured the avalanche wasn't very far above me and moving mighty damned fast.

I saddled up and rode down the creek. I stopped at Kerr's ranch, but I was told he had gone to Durango a couple of days before and was expected back any time. Luckily I met him on the road about a mile below his place.

I stopped, saying: "I've just been to your ranch to see you, Paul. I guess this is my lucky day."

He grinned. "Sure, Mark. Any day you see me is a lucky day, but I don't know if it's my lucky day seeing you. What law did I break?"

"None that I know of," I said, and told him what happened, and about my session with the other commissioners.

Kerr nodded sourly. "I heard about Catgut's strike before I left Durango. You're sure as hell right about what's going to happen." He scratched his long jaw, squinting at me, then added: "I don't agree with Joe and Frank about most things, but they're right as far as the county money goes. We just don't have any to pay a deputy, and we won't until the next budget is drawn up, which will be too late."

"You were here in the old days," I said. "You remember what Angel's Landing was like."

"I sure do," he said. "I've been in other tough camps, too. I don't want to see it happen here. Some good men will come in, but we'll have the scourings of hell, too. It'll overflow down here to my spread, so I'm as concerned as you are." He shook his head. "What do you aim to do?"

"I'm going to hire one man now," I answered. "I'll wait and see how it goes, but I know I'll have to hire more."

"You figure they'll work for nothing just for the privilege of packing a star?"

I laughed. "I wish they would. No, I'll pay them myself for a while, then I'll bill the county."

"You'd be wasting your time," he said. "You know and I know that I'm a permanent minority. The other two commissioners

45

represent the farmers in the west end of the county, and them farmers don't give a damn about what happens over here. On anything that costs them money, they care even less."

"I sure couldn't afford to pay my deputies very long," I said. "Maybe I'll just have to let the plug-uglies take the camp over and run it."

"No, Mark," he said. "You can't do that, either. The only suggestion I have is to talk your businessmen into raising the money themselves. I'll throw something into the kitty, and I'll talk to the others if you want me to."

I hadn't expected this from Paul Kerr, mostly because I hadn't figured that he'd see how much the lawlessness would affect him. I said: "Thanks, Paul. I may ask for your help. I had thought about trying that. It was my ace in the hole if nothing else worked. I'm just not sure we can raise that much money. If I'm guessing right, I'll need a big force of men before it's over."

"Who are you going to hire?"

"I'm going to try to get Tug Ralston," I answered. "I worked with him on the XL several years ago. He's a good man."

Kerr nodded. "He rode for me for a while. He is a good man. He might take the job. He's about to go under trying to run his ten-cow spread."

He nodded and rode on toward his place. For some reason I felt a hell of a lot better. Paul Kerr carried considerable weight in our end of the county. He might be able to help.

CHAPTER SEVEN

Tug Ralston was three years younger than I was. He was big and strong, and as independent as hell. During the time I worked with him, he was always talking about having his own spread. He never gambled; he didn't drink or smoke. Every nickel he could save went into the bank in Durango.

I had never met any other cowhand who had the drive Ralston did. After we drifted to other jobs, I heard he'd married a girl who had grown up on a shirt-tail spread south of Durango and had bought the Rafter B, a rundown little outfit a few miles down the creek from Kerr's spread.

I'd heard the same thing that Kerr had told me, that Ralston just didn't have the money to make a go of his ranch. The buildings needed repair, he had to buy more cattle and horses, and he had to have money to pay his hands. In the end he wound up doing the work himself and letting his hands go, and that meant losing stock and not having enough money to pay taxes and meet the bank interest.

In a way I hated to talk to him, but he was the only man I knew who could fill the bill, so I turned off the road and followed a lane that ran between two hay meadows to the Rafter B buildings. I hadn't been here for several years and everything looked a hell of a lot better than it had the last time I'd seen it.

The roofs of the buildings had been repaired. The house had been painted. There were white curtains at the windows and flowers in front of the house, and I could see a vegetable garden back of the woodshed. I had wondered what kind of a woman he'd married, but from the looks of things I'd have to say she was a good one.

Ralston was working on one of the corrals, so I reined over to him. He saw me coming and dropped his hammer. He yelled: "Well, by God, here comes the law!" He held up his hands. "Don't shoot. I surrender."

"Cut it out, Tug," I said as I stepped down. "I hear that kind of joke too often."

He laughed and held out his hand. "I'll bet you do, Mark. I guess it ain't funny to you. Come on into the house. The wife's probably got some hot coffee."

I shook my head. "I want to talk to you. If you're not interested, I'll ride on and there won't be no need to bother your wife."

He was a bigger man than I had remembered, taller than I am and heavier. When I had worked with him, he'd had a booming laugh and a friendly word no matter how much had happened. He'd been a happy man, but now I saw the nervous tic of a pulsating muscle in his cheek. Right then I began to doubt my own judgment and to wonder how much he'd changed.

He nodded toward the barn. "Let's go sit in the shade."

I left the reins dangling and walked with him to the splash of shade at the side of the barn. I told him about Catgut's strike and described how it had been in the boom days. He nodded. I knew he hadn't lived here then, but he'd heard the stories and knew what I was talking about.

"It's too bad," he said. "I mean, for us who live here. Most of us have liked this county the way it is. I don't cotton to crowds of people. I like 'em a few at a time. Of course I'm glad Catgut finally made his strike, but what's good for him ain't always good for the rest of us."

He dug his pipe out of his pocket, filled it, and fired it, scowling and shaking his head while he did it. "But you probably have heard about me. I ain't making it, Mark. I just didn't have enough capital to start with, and now I'm going to lose the whole shebang."

"I'd heard you were having trouble," I said. "I'm sorry. I remember how you used to dream about owning your own outfit."

"Yeah, I know I used to talk about it a lot," he said bitterly. "So I got myself the best woman in Colorado and the smartest and purtiest baby in the world, and now I'm gonna be broke by fall and I'll have to start over and try to support 'em on a cowhand's wages. I can't do it, Mark."

"I'm here to offer you a job," I said. "I don't know if you want to leave your outfit yet, but, if you do, you're the man I want. I need a deputy, a man I can trust and a man who's got the moxie and the guts to do the job."

He took his pipe out of his mouth and stared at me, then he laughed. "You're clean loco. I don't know nothing about being a lawman."

"Neither do I," I said, "but I'm going to learn fast in the next few days and I can't do the job by myself. I'll pay you fifty dollars a month and guarantee you four months' work. If the situation doesn't change, it'll be more."

He swallowed and kept staring at me. He asked: "You get that kind of money out of the county commissioners?"

"Not by a long shot," I said. "I'll pay you myself. I'll probably hire two or three more if it gets as bad as I think it will. Eventually Angel's Landing will incorporate and tax themselves to pay a town marshal, but that takes time and we don't have much time. I figure to get help raising money for my deputy's salaries, but right now I'll be responsible."

He held his cold pipe in his hand and stared beyond me at the red wall of the valley. Finally he said: "That's two hundred

49

cash dollars. Where would I live?"

"We can fix you a cot in the sheriff's office," I said. "There's a stove in it if you want to cook your meals. It won't cost you much to live."

"I can bring stuff from here," he said, paused, then added slowly: "I dunno if Sadie will live here by herself with the baby or not, and I hate like hell to ask her, but, if she would, we just might make it."

I could see the direction his thinking was taking him. I still didn't know what kind of a wife he had, but I didn't discourage the way he was leaning. He knew his wife. I wanted him, and, if he figured she could live here by herself, it was their business and I'd stay out of it.

I didn't say a word, but he rose, knocked his pipe out against his boot heel, slipped it into his pocket, and jerked his head at the house. "Let's go talk to Sadie," he said.

He led the way across the barnyard to the house, opened the screen door, and bawled: "Sadie! We've got company."

She came out of the kitchen, a big, raw-boned woman who was far from being a beauty, but she was pleasant and she looked competent. I liked her, and I made a guess that she'd say she could manage here by herself. I had a hunch she could, too.

Ralston introduced us, then said: "Fetch us some coffee. We've got to palaver."

"Why didn't you do your palavering where you were?" she asked.

"Because you're part of the palavering," he said. "Now get a move on."

"You married, Sheriff?" she asked.

"No."

"Well, when you get married, don't start ordering your wife around the way my husband does me," she said. "It won't work with most women. It wouldn't work with me if I wasn't so easy-going."

Tug snorted in derision and muttered: "Easy-going, you say?"

She winked at me and disappeared into the kitchen. I knew then that I had him. Sadie Ralston was capable and hard-working, and the feeling between them was right. I couldn't say that about most married couples I knew, but these two people were in love, they had the same goals, and it was my guess that there was nothing they wouldn't do for each other.

Ralston motioned to a battered leather chair. He said: "Sit down, Mark. We may be here a while."

His wife returned with two cups of steaming coffee. She gave one to me and one to Ralston, and, as she turned to sit down in a rawhide-bottom chair, he gave her a slap on her behind. She ignored it and nodded at me as she sat down.

"All right, Sheriff," she said. "Let's get the palavering over. I've got work to do."

I told her about Catgut's strike and what would certainly happen, and that I needed a deputy right away, then said: "I've offered Tug the job."

"Fifty dollars a month," he said eagerly, "and he's guaranteed me four months' work."

"You?" she demanded, as if she didn't believe what she'd heard. "You a deputy?" She scowled at me as if she didn't approve of the job, then added: "He'd make a good one, but it's risky work."

"It is, Missus Ralston," I said. "I sure wouldn't lie about it to you."

"I'd take a chance on that," he said, "but I reckon I can't go off and leave you here. I guess I'd have one day a week off when I could come home, wouldn't I?"

"Sure, unless we get into a tight situation," I said.

"It's up to you, Sadie," Ralston said. "You'd have to take care of the ranch and the house, but I reckon there ain't nothing outside you can't do. I want you to say how you feel about it. If you don't cotton to the notion, say so."

She was staring at Ralston, but I don't think she was seeing him at all. "Two hundred dollars," she said softly. "Two hundred dollars. With that much cash coming in by fall, we might stick it out for another year." Then she sort of stiffened. "Tug Ralston, are you asking me to live here for six days straight running while you're lollygagging in town with them outlaws and saloon girls?"

"I thought it might work . . . ," he began.

"All right," she interrupted, "I'll do it. I'll make out fine."

He looked at me and groaned. "That's the way she does." Then he grinned. "All right, Sadie. You've had your fun. If we can manage to hang on for another year, we'll know."

They were whipped. At least that was the way I saw it, though maybe nobody was beaten until he admitted it, and they weren't about to admit it. I finished my coffee, thinking that, if there was any justice, the Ralstons would keep their ranch, but the bank that held the mortgage would decide, and I'd never seen a bank that was overly concerned about justice.

"Thanks for the coffee," I said. "I've got to get back to town." Mrs. Ralston rose, and for a moment my eyes locked with hers. "You're a very unusual woman. I hope it works out for you."

"It will," she said. "It's got to. I'll tell you one thing, Sheriff. Tug don't know nothing about being a deputy, but he'll learn and he'll make you a good one."

"I figured he would," I said. "Can you start at the end of the week, Tug?"

He nodded. "I'll be there."

When I got back to town, I found that the kid I'd hired to work in the stable hadn't turned a hand. I gave him half a dollar and kicked his butt out through the archway. I went to work, and, just as I was finishing, Dutch Henry walked in.

"Well, I didn't figure I'd see you again," I said.

He looked as sheepish as hell. "There's an old Dutch proverb," he said, "that says a man's belly gives the orders. Can I have my job back?"

"You didn't find where Catgut made his strike?"

"No, but I reckon I didn't look very hard. I got to thinking about how many times I'd been hungry when I was prospecting and how many nights I damned near froze to death, and I kept thinking about you saying I hadn't been hungry since you gave me a job. Purty soon I knowed there wasn't enough gold in the world to make me go back to the way I used to live. I was rich twice and it didn't do me no good either time. You know, gold hunting is a fever and I'm cured."

I set the manure fork against the wall. "Go to the hotel and get your supper," I said. "You've got your old job back and this time you'd better keep it."

He raised a hand in salute. "Thank you kindly, sir. There's an old Dutch proverb that says, when you cast your bread upon the water, it comes back tenfold."

"Dutch proverb?" I yelled. "Get out of here before I take a pitchfork to you."

He disappeared. He'd get his belly full in the hotel dining room tonight, I thought, and I sure hoped this last proverb was right.

CHAPTER EIGHT

If Paul Kerr had heard about the strike, I figured others would have heard and they'd be along soon. I was right. For a few days we had only a trickle, mostly prospectors who had been in Durango and were wondering where to go next. In addition, a crew was sent to start working Catgut's claim. Another crew started widening the road through the Narrows. We could hear the dynamite blasts every day.

Dutch Henry borrowed a horse and rode up the cañon the third day. He came back, shaking his head. "Hell, I should have found it. Catgut was working behind some brush up one of the ravines and the brush was tall enough to hide what he'd been doing. He hadn't pushed the tunnel back more'n a few feet when he hit the vein. He quit right then and headed for town."

Henry threw up his hands. "You know, I could have been a millionaire just as well as old Catgut. I've found float in that same ravine and on down the cañon, but I never found the vein. Catgut wouldn't have, either, if that storm hadn't cleaned off the surface dirt and showed him enough of that vein to start him digging."

I wasn't so sure about Catgut being a millionaire. He hadn't showed up in Angel's Landing yet. I figured that, if he still owned the mine or even a part of it, he'd be out here bossing the job. Since he wasn't around, I figured he had sold out and left the country. Or, and this possibility bothered the hell out of me, he'd sold, the buyer had got him drunk, taken the money away from him, killed him, and hid his body. I didn't have a shred of evidence, so there wasn't anything I could do.

I asked Henry who was paying the miners. He gave me a questioning look, then he said: "That's the crazy part of it, Mark. I asked one of the men and he said the Lucky Cat Mine. I asked who owned it and he said he didn't know. Now if it was old Catgut, he'd have let everybody know who owned it."

By the end of the week the flood hit. The news had had time by then to fan out to the other camps in the San Juans, like Rico, Ouray, Telluride, and Silverton. None of them was doing much of anything, so the men who were living there were waiting to hear about the next strike. Banjo Creek was it.

The silver mines were practically all shut down and had been for several years. Cripple Creek was mining gold, so it was about the only camp in Colorado that was going full blast, but it didn't have enough jobs to keep every miner in the state busy.

The miners came on foot or horseback with their burros and gear. We had the usual crowd of saloon men, whores, pimps, and con men, along with legitimate businessmen. Sometimes it was hard to tell which was which. An active camp always attracts the scum who live off the men who work, and I knew it would be that bunch that would give me trouble.

Tug Ralston showed up on Saturday. I helped him get settled. He bought groceries, a cot, dishes, and pots and pans. We built shelves on one side of the sheriff's office for him. By evening we had the place pretty well fixed up.

"I'll buy your supper in the hotel dining room," I said, "and then we'll look around. Chances are it'll be a lively night for us."

It was. Before we finished eating, we began hearing gunshots. We were on our pie and the third cup of coffee when one of the bartenders Rip Yager had hired within the last week ran in and said there was a fight in Yager's Bar and two men were tearing the place up.

I never did get that last bite of pie. We left the dining room and fought our way through the mob on the street to Yager's Bar. Every building in town was occupied, and tents had been set up at both ends of the business block. Judging from the crowd, I guessed that all the men who had gone up Banjo Creek in the last week had showed up in Angel's Landing to turn their wolves loose.

A couple of big bruisers who were just drunk enough to be mean were tearing up the tables and chairs in Yager's Bar. Tug and I stopped inside the batwings for a moment and watched them. It seemed to me they were more intent on tearing up the place than on fighting.

Rip was dancing around with a shotgun in his hands, yelling at them to stop, but they weren't paying any attention. I had always pegged Rip for a tough hand, and maybe he had been at one time, but he sure didn't have the guts to use his scatter-gun. If we hadn't got there when we did, he wouldn't have had a saloon.

"Take the red beard, Tug," I said. "I'll handle the bald-headed bastard."

We pulled our guns and bulled our way through the ring of men who were watching the show. I didn't try to palaver. I didn't figure it would do any more good than Rip's yelling. I grabbed Baldy by a shoulder, yanked him around, and cracked him on the head with my gun barrel.

The fellow folded at knees and hip and spilled out full length on the floor. When I looked around, I saw that Tug had done the same with Redbeard. Neither man was out cold, but we had taken the fight out of them.

I toed my man in the ribs. "On your feet, bucko," I said. "You're going to jail. We've got a couple of cells that'll fit both of you just fine."

The crowd started to growl.

I let the men see the muzzle of my Colt. "Any of you boys want to pick this up?" I asked. "We've got room for all of you."

One of them, a squat, barrel-chested man, said: "You're damned right we'll pick this up. Toting a star don't make you God. I've seen the likes of you in every camp I've been in. You ain't as big as you're making out you are."

He started toward me, his big fists swinging. Some of the others fell in behind him. I didn't have time to think what I should do, but I did know that this was the kind of situation I'd been afraid I'd fall into. I also knew that Tug and I couldn't handle fifty men, that they'd tear us apart if we let them, and that, if I didn't make my authority stick now, I was finished as a lawman in Angel's Landing before I got started.

"Don't push it, mister," I said, cocking my gun.

He cursed me and said he was going to lock me up in my own jail. He kept coming, so I shot him in the foot. He screamed bloody murder and sprawled on the floor. The others dropped back in a hurry, staring at me as if they didn't believe I'd really done it.

I called to Yager: "Get Doc!" I kicked Baldy in the ribs again. "On your feet," I said. "You're going to jail." This time he obeyed.

Tug had Redbeard on his feet, too. We marched them out of the saloon, the crowd opening up before us. The squat man was on the floor, squirming around and yelling that I'd crippled him for life and he was bleeding to death.

A crowd had gathered outside, but nobody tried to interfere. We took our prisoners to the county jail and locked each one in the small cells, the first time I'd used them since I'd pinned on the star. Then we stepped back into the sheriff's office.

Tug wiped his sweaty face with his bandanna and stared at

me. He said in a low tone: "We're still alive, but we wouldn't be, if you hadn't shot that son-of-a-bitch."

"I never shot a man before in my life," I said. "I didn't think I could do it."

"You know one thing for sure now," he said. "You need more men."

I nodded. "It'll get worse before it gets better, but knowing I need the men doesn't give me the money to hire them. Well, we'd better stay together the rest of the night. If just one of us had walked into Yager's Bar, it would have been a hell of a lot worse than it was."

We patrolled the business block until midnight, then I told Tug to go to bed and that he could take Sunday off since it would be the quietest day of the week. The men who had raised hell half the night would be sleeping off their headaches most of Sunday.

Yager's Bar closed at 1:00 A.M. I stepped through the batwings just before Rip locked up. He was still there with his two bartenders, but the customers were gone. We had arrested several men for drunkenness, but we'd picked them up on the street. I'd made a point to stay away from Yager. I should have stayed away longer than I did. The minute he saw me, he started in on me about driving business away.

I stood it as long as I could, then I said: "Rip, you can shut your mouth. You had a shotgun. You could have stopped the row before we got here. If you didn't want us to stop it, why did you send for us?"

"I didn't want you to shoot nobody," he said sullenly. "That's where you made your mistake."

"What did you want me to do, stand there and let them beat us to death?" I demanded. "I didn't make a mistake, Rip. That's exactly what they would have done, and for no reason except that we were the law. Chances are they'd have turned on you. They were drunk and mean and ready to tear the town apart. That's what we've got on our hands, Rip, and we'll have it every Saturday night. We've got to keep the lid on."

"They won't come to town on Saturday nights and spend their money if they think they're gonna get shot," he snapped. "Mark, we've got to bring in a professional. You and Tug are cowboys. You ain't town tamers."

"I don't aim to tame this town," I said. "I just want to keep it from being destroyed."

I stood there, staring at him, an old man I had known since I was ten years old, a man I had always liked and respected. Now he was different. He acted as if I had injured him.

Then I thought I understood. He was just plain greedy. If the Lucky Cat strike didn't play out the way the gravel on Banjo Creek had in the old days, Rip had a chance to make big money for the first time in eighteen years. He'd rather have his saloon torn up than to lose business. He was being about as short-sighted as a man could be, but I'd seen plenty of such examples in other men. Rip had been satisfied with a little business all these years, but now he figured this was his last chance to make it big. In one way he was like Catgut Dolan.

He couldn't look at me. He muttered: "A professional. That's what we need."

I thought to hell with him, wheeled around, and walked out. I should have known what he was up to, but I didn't. Not for another week.

CHAPTER NINE

I slept late Sunday morning. It was close to noon by the time I dressed and built a fire. When I went to the woodpile back of the house to saw enough wood to cook breakfast, I noticed that Abbie Trevor had left the teacherage and was coming toward my place.

I laid a log on the sawhorse and sawed off a block, then straightened up and called: "Good morning, Abbie!"

"Good morning, Mark," she said as she came up to me. "You must have been busy last night."

"I was," I said.

"What was all the shooting about?"

I didn't want to tell her I'd shot a man, so I shrugged and said: "A bunch of miners letting off steam."

"I came over to cook breakfast for you," she said.

"That's the kind of offer I never turn down," I said. "I'll bring some wood in for you. I've got to go to the jail, but I won't be gone long."

She nodded and disappeared into the house. By the time I had split the wood and carried an armload into the kitchen, she had the coffee pot on the stove and was stirring up a batch of biscuits.

"I'll be right back," I said, grabbing my gun belt off the antler rack near the door and buckling it around me as I hurried out of the house.

I thought Tug Ralston would be gone and I'd have a jail full of drunks nursing king-size headaches, but I found Tug swamping out an empty cell.

"I thought you'd be gone," I said.

He threw a bucket of dirty water into the yard in front of the jail and wiped a sleeve across his face. It was hot already. By late afternoon the small cells would be overheated ovens.

"I couldn't go off and leave that cell like it was," he said. "Them bastards were yelling and carrying on and singing until about sunup. I didn't sleep much."

I could still smell the puke and urine. I said: "It must have been a mess."

"I've got hogs at home that are better specimens of the human race than the things we locked up last night," he said in disgust. "I didn't turn loose the two we cracked on the head. I didn't know if you wanted to hold 'em for the judge or not."

I shook my head. "Rip chewed my head off last night for shooting a man. He's afraid he'll lose his business after it gets around that the sheriff shoots his customers."

"Hell, if you hadn't . . . ," Tug began, and then stopped. "After this we can let 'em tear his place down. That fellow you shot, Ten-Sleep Morgan, you know anything about him?"

"No. Just another miner who doesn't like law officers, I guess."

"No he ain't," Tug said. "That's the point. He wanted to be taken for a miner, I reckon, and maybe he has been working somewhere up in the cañon, but, according to one of the men we jailed last night, he really works for Ben Scully."

"Scully?" I had to think a moment, and then I remembered he was the gambler and saloonkeeper who had put up a big tent at the south end of Main Street. He'd had a bar going last night along with several poker tables and some other games, but his place hadn't been fully staffed. He had promised that in another week it would be.

I began adding things up. I said: "I guess it wasn't just a case of this Ten-Sleep Morgan hating lawmen. He was trying to bust us up the first week Scully was in town . . . then Scully would have the camp to himself."

"That's the way I figured it," Tug said. "Well, I'll be sloping out of here."

"You don't have to come back until Monday night," I said.

"Thanks. I can sure use the extra time at home."

I unlocked the two small cells and told Redbeard and Baldy to be on their way. "You might see Rip Yager before you leave town," I said. "You busted several of his tables and chairs last night. I don't know if he'll hand you a bill for them or not."

They were hurting from the head cracking we'd given them, along with hangovers, but they weren't hurting so much they forgot to threaten me. "We'll be back," Redbeard said, "and we'll finish you and that smart aleck deputy of yours."

"Ben Scully ain't done with you, neither," Baldy said. "Ten-Sleep won't be getting around much and Ben needs him."

"Git," I said. "You raise hell again and I'll jail you till Judge Manders has his next session of court."

I walked back to my house, about as worried as I'd ever been in my life. It was my guess that the whole row in Yager's Bar had been staged, that Redbeard and Baldy both worked for Scully. It was hard enough to handle a town running over with miners who were looking for trouble; it was twice as tough to buck a man like Scully who wanted to discredit the law. I didn't know a thing about Ben Scully, but it was a good guess that he wanted a wide-open camp, and that was the one thing I didn't aim to have.

Abbie had breakfast ready when I reached the house. She sat down across from me and sipped a cup of coffee while I ate. She said: "When are you going to irrigate the garden, Mark? It's awfully dry."

"This afternoon," I said. "I've got to see a man when I get done with breakfast, but I'll take care of it as soon as I get back."

"I've been afraid you'd forget your promise," she said. "It doesn't take long for the ground to dry out when we get a hot spell like this. Everything's up and looking good."

"I'll do it," I said, "unless there's a riot or an act of God."

"We had that when the storm hit," she said.

I looked at her, suddenly seeing her in a different light than I had before. She was an uncommonly pretty woman. Funny I'd never noticed it before. I had always considered her plain, but now she was wearing a frilly, pink-and-white-checked dress, she had curled her hair, and her cheeks were pink. She must have used some rouge, I thought, and that was about the last thing I expected of her, but it did wonders for her.

"You're very pretty this morning, Abbie," I said.

She blushed and looked down at her cup of coffee. She said: "Mark, that's the first time you ever said that."

"I guess I've taken you for granted," I said, "but I won't from now on."

She smiled. "Thank you, Mark. No woman likes to be taken for granted."

All of a sudden I saw the light. I said: "I guess that was what you meant when you told me that if I didn't know why you couldn't marry me, you couldn't tell me."

"That's right," she said. "That's exactly right. A woman wants to know that the man she's marrying loves her and considers her important. That's where your father made his mistake. I'm sure he loved your mother, but not enough to make her the most important part of his life. Chasing the rainbow was more important to him than she was."

"That's right," I said, "but you've got to understand that there will be times when I'll have to pay more attention to other things than to you."

"Of course," she said quickly. "I realize that your duties as sheriff may take most of your time for a while, but I know now how you feel about me. That was what held me back. I just didn't know."

I kept my mouth shut. The truth was I didn't know what to say, and I certainly had no idea what I'd done or said that had proved to her how I felt about her, but I was damned if I was going to ask. I was stupid enough about women, without letting her know just how stupid I actually was.

She didn't say anything else until I finished my breakfast. She sat staring at her empty coffee cup. I don't know if she sensed what I was thinking or not, but presently she said: "It isn't so much what a man says to a woman that counts . . . it's what he does. When we had the storm, you showed me how you felt. If you'd tried to . . . well, I mean, there is a correct time for everything."

"Sure," I said. "That's right."

I knew what she meant, of course, and I likewise knew she was making something out of my actions that hadn't been there, but I wasn't going to hurt her by setting her right.

Sometimes I wondered about my feelings for her. Perhaps I had sort of fallen into this situation, knowing her as long as I had and feeling comfortable with her. Actually I wasn't sure that I could recognize love if I fell into it. All I knew was that I liked Abbie, and I was sure we could have a good life together. That wasn't enough for her, and maybe it wouldn't have been enough for any woman.

If I married her, I was going to have to fool her, something my father had never been willing to do for my mother. He'd had a crazy, stiff-necked pride that I didn't have, so I could, I thought, marry her and make her happy.

Then I remembered Ben Scully and I got a little scared. He'd been in situations like this before, and he knew how to handle them, and, having no morals, he could and would do anything he needed to do to accomplish his goal. I guess I'm like most people—guilty of putting off things I don't want to do or am afraid to do, so I put off seeing Scully.

I rose. I said: "I guess I'll do the irrigating first and see the man later."

She rose, too, and came around the table to me. She put her arms around me and kissed me, and then tipped her head back and looked at me. She said: "Something's worrying you, Mark. Tell me about it."

I decided to tell her what had happened last night and what I was going to do, then I said: "I need to think about it a little more. I haven't made up my mind what to say to him."

She began to tremble. "Mark, let's get married right away. I'd never forgive myself if we put it off too long."

I didn't agree. I couldn't bring myself to marry her now and run the risk of getting killed and leaving her pregnant. Still, I didn't want to argue with her, so I said: "We won't put it off very long, Abbie. I promise."

I spent most of the afternoon irrigating the garden, using more time than I needed to. I got tired and hot, and then I got mad, just plain, down right sore all the way to my boot heels. He'd set me up, aiming to kill me or cripple me for life. I'd be a fool to let him get away with it. I knew then what I was going to say and do. I went into the house, washed up, changed my shirt, and headed for Scully's saloon.

CHAPTER TEN

When I first went into Ben Scully's tent, I thought it was empty. After I'd taken a couple of steps, I stopped to give my eyes time to adjust to the gloom after being out in the bright sunshine, and then I saw a bartender standing behind the rough pine bar.

Beyond the bartender near the rear of the tent, Ben Scully was sitting at a desk working on his books. Ten-Sleep Morgan sat a few feet from him, his bandaged foot resting on a chair in front of him, a pair of crutches propped against the chair.

I felt a strong temptation to turn around and walk out and leave it up to Scully to make the next move. If I'd waited about half a minute, I'd have given in to that temptation. I was that scared, so I knew I couldn't wait. I headed straight for Scully's desk, thinking that, if I let him make the next move, I'd be dead.

Morgan watched me come up, an amused expression on his ugly face. Scully pointedly ignored me until I stopped beside his desk, then he looked up, smiled, and said: "What can I do for you, Sheriff?"

He was a handsome son-of-a-bitch. About forty, I judged, tall and slender, with a carefully trimmed dark mustache and long, equally dark sideburns. He wore a black Prince Albert coat, white silk shirt, and string tie.

Glancing down, I saw a huge diamond ring on his right hand, which he had placed palm down on the desk top.

I had the impression that Ben Scully was a perfect example

of the inscrutable gambler. His light blue eyes told me nothing. He didn't even appear amused, as Morgan did. The smile was fastened on his lips, a forced smile, as if he was a little bored and was simply waiting for me to get the hell out of there so he could get on with his bookkeeping. Somehow he contrived to give the impression that he controlled his destiny and the destiny of the entire camp, a total arrogance I had never seen before in any man.

Then I thought about how it had been in Yager's Bar, how this bastard had set the scene for my murder, and a crazy kind of pinwheeling explosion burst across my mind. Afterward, I was never sure how or why it happened because I was not a man to give way to sudden flashes of temper. All I'm sure of is that I never gave a thought to the consequences.

I reached out with my right foot, hooked the toe of my boot under Ten-Sleep Morgan's chair and yanked it out from under him. He spilled to the ground in a sprawling fall and must have landed on his wounded foot because he let out a howl of pain you could have heard in the other end of town.

Scully swore and jerked a drawer of his desk open, but he never got his hand on his gun. I grabbed him by the shoulders and hauled him to his feet and hit him on the jaw. It was a hell of a good punch that started below my waist and connected perfectly. He threw his hands up and fell full length on his back and lay motionless.

I pulled my gun and wheeled on the bartender just as he was bringing a sawed-off shotgun out from behind the bar. I said: "Go ahead, mister. I feel like killing somebody and it might as well be you. I'll work up to Scully."

He glared at me, his mouth dropping open, spit running down his chin, then he swiped a sleeve across his face and carefully set the shotgun on the bar.

I said: "Well now, you figure you want to live a while?"

"That's right," he said. "I ain't fixing to die for Ben Scully today."

"Good," I said. "Now fetch a bucket of water and see if you can bring Scully back to life."

He picked up a bucket, walked to Scully, and emptied it on the man's head, then strode back to the bar. I turned so that my back was to the wall of the tent near the rear opening. From where I stood I could watch all three men. Morgan was sitting up, his gaze on me. He was absolutely furious, but he carefully refrained from making any hostile move.

"You ain't satisfied to shoot my foot off," he said in an outraged tone. "You've got to dump me on the same damned foot."

"It's not my fault if you fall on the wrong foot," I said, "but I'm wondering what I'd have fallen on if you'd made your play good last night."

Scully was sitting up, making gurgling sounds and swiping at his face. The front of his shirt and coat were soaking wet, but I had a feeling, when I looked at him, that there was a trace of admiration in his eyes.

"I figured you were making a peaceful call, Sheriff," Scully said. "Otherwise, we'd have been ready for you. Would you mind telling me why we're getting acquainted this way?"

"You're an ignorant man, Scully," I said, "so I guess I'll have to educate you with a little information. You set up me and my deputy in Yager's Bar last night, aiming to kill us or bust us up so bad that we wouldn't have any fight left in us and that we'd leave it up to you to run the camp any way you want to. Now I'll explain the situation. You try it again and you're leaving Angel's Landing, bag and baggage."

He didn't deny my accusation. He got up, a hand feeling carefully of his jaw, and sat down at his desk. "All right," he said. "It won't happen again. Not from me, anyhow. I'm aiming to make a big investment in this camp. I'll put up a good building that will contain a fine saloon and gambling layout. I'll have girls and music and the best liquor in Angel's Landing. You need that kind of place, so don't run me out of camp."

He paused, his eyes narrowing, then added: "For a clodhopper sheriff who don't know nothing about enforcing the law, you cut quite a swath. You don't care whether you make any enemies or not."

"I'd rather have enemies I know about than step into the kind of trap I almost stepped into last night," I said. "Now have I made myself clear?"

"Very clear, Sheriff," Scully said.

I stepped out through the rear opening of the tent, not holstering my gun until I was back on Main Street. As I walked home, I had an absolutely crazy feeling that Ben Scully and I were going to be friends.

When Tug Ralston got back Monday evening, I told him about it. He laughed and said: "Clodhopper sheriff, are you? I guess that makes me a clodhopper deputy."

I shook my head. "I dunno, Tug. He's right about one thing. I sure don't know much about enforcing the law."

"Neither do I," he said, "but you told me I'd make a good deputy. Looks to me like it's a case of us learning our business. I'll tell you something else. You've got the right instincts for the job, just like a hound dog has got the right instincts for hunting."

I was glad to hear Tug say that. I'd had too many doubts about myself ever since I'd left Scully's tent. I had begun to think that I wasn't man enough for the job simply because I wasn't sure I'd handled Scully right.

My last doubt was dispelled the following morning when Scully came into the livery stable where I was working with Dutch Henry. We'd been busier than the proverbial cat on a tin roof. I'd even hired the boy back that I'd fired a few days before because I didn't know anyone else I could get. The kid was better than nothing as long as Dutch Henry or I was there to tell him what to do.

I leaned on the manure fork as Scully picked his way along the runway to where I stood. I kept my right hand close to the butt of my gun because I just wasn't sure what he was up to. He didn't have the slightest hint of a smile on his face as he extended his hand.

"No hard feelings, Sheriff?" Scully asked.

"Not as long as you behave yourself," I said as I shook hands with him.

"I'll behave myself as far as you're concerned," he said. "You convinced me you can hold up your end of things. I didn't think so before. That was why I wanted you out of the way. I've gone through more boom and bust camps than you can count and I've learned how to play the game. I won't make any promises about how I'll behave as far as my competition is concerned. You see, there's one ace I insist on holding. I aim to see that the local law is in the hands of a good sheriff or marshal."

He was a fastidious man and the smell of horse manure was a little more than he could stand. The expression on his face was one of actual pain and I wondered if he'd throw his boots away after leaving the stable.

"You figure I'm your ace?" I asked.

"That's right," he said. "I don't want to invest my money in a good building and hire the girls and dealers I'll need if a mob is going to run this camp. That's why I'm here this morning. No matter how good you and your deputy are, you can't ramrod a camp as big as this one's going to be. My men, like Ten-Sleep, will help you if there's an emergency, but you need at least two more good deputies. I want you to hire them."

I shook my head and told him how it was with the county commissioners and that I was paying Tug Ralston out of my own pocket.

He swore and threw up his hands. "That's like a couple of jackleg farmers. I know Paul Kerr. He's a reasonable man."

"Sure," I agreed, "but don't forget he's only one man out of three."

"I know," he said. "It'll take time to incorporate and we don't have that much time. There is one other thing you can do. The commissioners ought to agree because it will give the county money. They could require every saloon and whorehouse to pay a license fee. One hundred dollars annually would be about right. That would give the county enough to pay the salaries of a dozen deputies."

"It's a good idea," I said. "I'm going to Durango this afternoon to bring back a new buggy. I'll stop at Kerr's ranch and talk to him, but you know what will happen. Those two bastards will use the money for something else."

He nodded. "You might be right, but it's the only thing I can think of."

He wheeled and minced his way back down the runway. I figured he'd get a good, long breath of fresh air once he was back on the street.

I left right after dinner, stopped at Kerr's place on my way south, and mentioned the license idea. He agreed that it might be the answer and promised he'd write to the other commissioners about it.

I went on to Durango and got back to Angel's Landing after dark. One thing was sure—I had to invest in more rigs and horses. Crowds of men were coming in every day, a few with families, but most of them were single men who either went on up Banjo Creek, aiming to stake out claims, or who were looking for work in town. A few actually had money and had come to investigate the business opportunities that were here.

Freight wagons rolled in every day, many loaded with lumber. It seemed to me that each minute of the daylight hours was punctuated by the pounding of hammers and the scream of saws. A brick building across the street from Yager's Bar was being renovated and was scheduled to open soon as the Angel's Landing State Bank.

We had a drugstore, a jewelry store, a millinery shop, and half a dozen new saloons along with a bunch of whorehouses that for the time being were located in tents. Some of the newcomers were con men, professional gamblers, and pimps, and others were just plain sneak thieves.

Tug and I ran some of them out of town, but more came. I talked to Scully about it and he said I could expect this kind of scum, but that they didn't make a real threat. They were like mosquitoes; they could be handled. What I had to watch out for were the organization men who worked together and would try to take over the camp if it got big enough to be worth their trouble.

I knew what had happened in Leadville and what Soapy Smith had done in Creede. I told Scully that, if he got wind of anything like that, to let me know. I was convinced now that Ben Scully would work with me and could be depended on.

The week was quiet enough. We had our hands full again on Saturday night, but we stayed on top of it. By midnight we had the jail full. If the camp got any bigger, we'd have to find more space to hold the drunks who could be dangerous if they were allowed to roam around town.

I thought we had done a good job. Then, on Sunday afternoon when Angel's Landing was so quiet you'd have thought the town was deserted, old Rip Yager threw his bombshell.

CHAPTER ELEVEN

Abbie spent Sunday morning working in the garden, hoeing and thinning the vegetables. Spring always came late at our altitude, but when the warm weather came, every kind of plant seemed to try to outdo the others. The radishes particularly were coming fast.

When I returned to the house from the livery stable, Abbie had dinner almost ready. I kissed her and she asked: "When are we getting married, Mark?"

"Getting impatient?"

"A little." She laughed, then sobered, and added gravely: "No, it's just that I get a funny feeling sometimes that we're waiting too long, that something's going to happen to you. If it does, I want to be married."

I sat down at the table. Abbie brought me a cup of coffee. I sat there, sipping it, knowing that Abbie expected me to say something. I was afraid to tell her the truth, but I finally decided I'd better.

"I'm impatient, too, Abbie," I said, "and I've got that same feeling. It's kind of like having a nightmare. You know you're in danger but you can't wake up enough to ward it off. I feel cornered. I've got a bear by the tail and I can't let go. I just had no way of knowing what was going to happen when I agreed to run for sheriff."

She came to the table and put an arm around my shoulder. "I know. I stay up on Saturday nights until I see a light in your house and I know you're back and safe. It's more than I can stand to have you walking the street and arresting drunks. There's bound to be one who'll get drunk enough to want to kill a lawman." Her grip tightened on my shoulder. "We can't wait for men like Rip Yager to give you the help you need. Let's get married tomorrow."

I looked up at her. I could not understand how this plain-faced schoolteacher could have become a beautiful woman in a few weeks, but it had happened and I was glad she was going to be my wife.

I knew then I had to say it, all of it. "Abbie, I know how my mother scrambled and scrounged around raising me after my father went sashaying off to find gold. I won't put you through that, not until our situation has shaped up and I know I can live a reasonable life and have the help I need. I can't resign now that I'm into this business, and I won't run a chance of getting killed and leaving you pregnant. The way it stands now, I'll be a dead man in a month."

She turned away and I thought she was crying, but she did not let herself break down. Finally she said: "I'd rather have it that way than not to ever have you, Mark. I've waited so long."

I told her about Ben Scully and his idea of the county charging a license fee. "Maybe I'll get the help I need," I said. "If I do, we'll get married."

She nodded and let it go at that. I spent most of the afternoon irrigating, and all the time the pressure of what I expected to happen kept weighing on me. I knew what we'd have in a few weeks. I could not logically expect any help from the county, and I certainly could not afford to pay a second man's salary.

If it was up to me and Tug Ralston, we'd simply be swept under. I could expect some help from Scully, but not enough. I simply could not turn my back on the trouble that was bound to pile up until it became an avalanche, roaring down on top of me. Sooner or later I'd have men like Ten-Sleep Morgan gunning for me, and sooner or later one of them would get me. Pride is a hell of a powerful force in a man. To save my life, I could not walk away from the sheriff's job.

I was just finishing irrigating when one of Rip Yager's bartenders came around the house, saw me, and called: "Rip wants to see you right away!"

I straightened up and looked at the man, so damned mad to think that Yager would order me to come to him that I almost let his bartender have both barrels, but I realized that he was simply obeying orders.

"If Rip wants to see me, he knows where I live," I said.

"He's having a meeting," the man said. "He's sent for Kirk Bailey, Doc Jenner, and Joe Steele. He says it's important."

I leaned on my shovel handle and thought about it. I didn't like it one bit, remembering Rip's attitude when he cussed me out for shooting a man who would have killed me if I'd let him. Rip had changed in the last few weeks. I hadn't seen much of the others, but they were all making more money than they had ever made. Right then I had a hunch they'd changed, too.

"All right," I said. "I'll be there."

I went into the house, changed my sweaty shirt for a clean one, and washed up. When I got to Yager's Bar, I saw that it was deserted except for some cowboys who were playing poker at one of the tables. Except for two strange bartenders, Yager's Bar was exactly the way it would have been before Catgut made his strike.

The bartender who had come for me jerked a thumb at the back room. He said: "They're waiting for you."

I nodded and crossed the room. I opened the door, stepped into the room, and shut the door behind me. They were sitting there, all right, all four of them, and I had a hunch they had been there for a while and had been talking about me.

75

They sure as hell had changed. I sensed a hostility from them, something I had never felt before from any of them until I'd shot Ten-Sleep Morgan, and then only from Yager. I had considered these men my friends, but now I knew damned well they weren't. A prickle ran down my spine and I thought of my conversation at noon with Abbie. Something was up and I didn't like the smell of it.

Rip motioned toward a chair. I pulled it back from the table and sat down. I filled my pipe, fired it, and puffed for a moment. No one said anything for a time. I had a feeling they were uncomfortable, Rip particularly, and the other three were waiting for him to start talking.

Finally I said: "Well, Rip, did you send for me to cuss me out again for stopping a couple of men from tearing your place up and for shooting a man who wanted to kill me?"

"No, I'm willing to let that go." He looked at the others, then cleared his throat and brought his gaze back to me. "There is something else we wanted to talk about. We used to call ourselves the town council. I guess there are a few others who would like to be included, but we've been here a long time and I think we've got a right to decide some things."

"Like what?" I asked.

"Well, like keeping the peace," Yager said. "I told you the other day that we needed a professional lawman."

I'd had a hunch what he was driving at; now there wasn't any doubt, and it made me sore. I demanded: "Just what's wrong with the way Tug and I are keeping the peace?"

"Nothing now," Yager said, "but you know as well as I do that this is only the beginning. Angel's Landing is going to be a big camp. The company that's developing the Lucky Cat Mine is figuring on putting up a mill in Banjo Cañon and there's been another strike above where Catgut made his. It ain't a big one, but it's a promising vein and they're going to follow up on it.

That means another payroll. We need an experienced man who knows how to handle the kind of cussedness that we're bound to get in a big camp."

I didn't know about the mill and I hadn't heard about the new strike, and I had to admit there was some sense in what he was saying, but I was still sore. I knew damned well that, if I had the deputies, I could keep the peace. These men weren't even willing to help pay Tug's salary.

I said: "It seems to me that you might give me some help instead of trying to get rid of me and Tug."

"Oh, hell," Doc Jenner said. "It's not a matter of getting rid of you. As a matter of fact, you two will have all you can do to keep things under control out in the county. What we want is a town marshal who'll ride herd on Angel's Landing."

"Who's paying him?" I asked.

"We'll all chip in," Bailey said. "We'll ask every businessman to help out."

"Then you can chip in on Tug Ralston's pay," I said. "Right now it's coming out of my pocket."

"You made the deal with Tug and you can pay it," Yager said tartly. "We aim to hire a tough marshal and we want you to deputize him."

I could feel my temper skidding out of control, not so much because of what they were saying, but because of the way they had done it. They sure hadn't invited me to their meeting, and now they were telling me what to do.

"Just where do you figure to find a man like that?" I asked. "The tough lawmen like Wyatt Earp and Bill Hickock are dead or retired."

Yager shook his head. "Not quite. Captain John Wallace is alive, he is not retired, and he is available. I've sent for him."

My temper quit skidding. It was paralyzed. My gaze moved from Yager to Doc Jenner and on to Bailey and finally to Steele.

They all looked a little uneasy, maybe a little ashamed, and more than anything else, just plain scared.

"You know anything about Wallace?" I asked finally.

Yager nodded. "I met him in Leadville when he was a peace officer there. I know his record."

I doubted that. If he had, he wouldn't have sent for him. I said: "He must be about a hundred years old. He goes back to Hickock's time."

"No, he's in his fifties," Yager said. "He was in his early twenties when he started in Dodge City."

I took a long breath. I said: "Before I tell you what I think of what you've done, I want to know if you've done this out of ignorance or what. You know that Wallace is not really a lawman. He's a gunman, a murderer who has gone unpunished because he's always been able to hide behind his star. I doubt that he knows how many men he's killed."

"We didn't invite him out of ignorance," Doc Jenner said sharply. "We know his record. Rip says it's exaggerated."

Yager leaned forward and said: "Mark, we want a man who has the kind of reputation that will help him keep the peace. Wallace has that kind of reputation. Everybody knows about him and they'll be afraid to get drunk in town. We have made him an offer for one month. After that, the riff-raff will be gone and we can let him go."

"You're a good cowboy," Doc Jenner said patronizingly. "So is Tug, but that doesn't make either one of you good law officers. You took the sheriff's job because you had time and you lived here, so we urged you to run. You didn't bargain for the kind of job it's turned out to be." He waggled a forefinger at me. "We don't want Angel's Landing run by some con man like Soapy Smith ran Creede."

Ben Scully had called me a clodhopper sheriff. Maybe I was and maybe Tug Ralston fitted the same description, but we'd done our best, we'd risked our lives, we had kept the peace, and I was damned sure that no Soapy Smith was going to run Angel's Landing.

"You've lost something," I said. "All four of you. We had something good here, peace and harmony and nobody wanting more than his share, but now you're in it for all you can get. You're as bad as Rip, who got sore because I arrested two men who were tearing up his place and because I shot a man who aimed to kill me."

They got red in the face. Doc Jenner said harshly: "Angel's Landing wasn't what it is now. It's not our fault that Catgut Dolan made his strike, but he did, and now it's our job to handle the problems that he gave us."

That was sorry reasoning to explain sending for a man like Captain John Wallace. It struck me that Doc Jenner was the leader, the one who was responsible for bringing Wallace here, and I remembered how often I had heard him say that he liked things just the way they were, that he didn't make much money, but then he didn't need much.

I couldn't be sure what had changed his mind, but I knew he owned a good deal of property in town and I also knew that every lot was skyrocketing in price. He could make a fortune if he could maintain what investors would call law and order, and to hell with the little man who got hurt. They would get hurt if Wallace was running the camp, but Doc Jenner would have sold his lots by that time.

Suddenly I realized I was pussyfooting, and then my temper skidded clear out of control. I looked Jenner right in the eyes and said: "Gentlemen, you didn't see fit to take me into your confidence, but I'll take you into mine. By God, I'll see all of you in hell before I deputize John Wallace."

I wheeled and strode out of the saloon, and I swear that, if

79

CHAPTER TWELVE

I started home, thinking about Captain John Wallace and trying to recall what I knew about the man. He had become a legend in much the way that Wyatt Earp and Doc Holliday had, and for much the same reason. He was, as I told Yager and the others, a killer who hid behind a badge and therefore had been immune to arrest for murder.

According to the stories I'd read or heard, Wallace had learned to kill during the Civil War when he'd ridden with Quantrill. There was some talk that he'd hooked up with the James and Younger gangs, though I'm not sure that it was ever proved. He drifted West before he ended up the way Jesse James had and served as marshal in several cow towns like Dodge City and Abilene.

Wallace must have known the famous ones like Wild Bill Hickock and Bat Masterson, but I never heard of him fighting any of them. Somehow he managed to outlive most of his contemporaries. I wasn't sure whether he was not as fast with his gun as a man like Hickock, or whether he had a way of avoiding trouble with such men. The ones he killed were unknowns, and I suspected most of them were kids trying to make a reputation for themselves by knocking over a famous gunman.

What I'd heard about Wallace were fragments that got into the newspapers when he had a gunfight, so I'm sure there was a good deal about him I didn't know. I'd read that he had, like others of his stripe, come on West to Colorado and had served as a lawman in mining camps like Leadville, where Rip Yager had known him.

I also had heard that he'd been in the Black Hills for a while, and then had gone to Montana, where he had spent time in Miles City when it had been a booming cow town, but I hadn't heard anything about him for a long time. I had assumed he'd ended up like so many others of his caliber, that he'd met a man who was faster with a gun than Captain John Wallace.

I was almost to my house when I reached a decision that turned me around and sent me back to Main Street. I needed to know more about Wallace and it struck me that Ben Scully could tell me. He did, too, more than I wanted to know.

I found Scully working on his books just as I had the previous Sunday. Ten-Sleep Morgan was sitting across from him, his foot still bandaged. The only difference was that two women were with Scully. I'd never had much to do with whores. I knew there were some you would never recognize for what they were, but I had no trouble with these two. They were overdressed, over-painted, and over-used.

Scully greeted me with a friendly handshake. Even Morgan shook hands with me. Then Scully introduced me to the women. He called them Dolly and Daisy. They giggled and fauned around as if they thought I'd come in to do business with them. Scully said they were using two tents behind his big one. He expected to start construction on his building the following Monday and the women would have rooms upstairs.

"My building will be a credit to Angel's Landing," he said. "I figure on living here a while, so I'm not going to do anything to cheapen the camp. I expect this place to grow. You heard about the new strike up Banjo Creek?"

I nodded. "I also heard that the people who are working the Lucky Cat Mine are figuring on putting up a mill."

He shook his head. "I hadn't heard that, but I doubt that they'll do it. They might just as well haul the ore to Durango. We may get a railroad spur up here. That would beat building a new mill since they already have one in Durango." He motioned toward a chair. "Sit down, Sheriff. What can I do for you?"

"I came for information and advice," I said.

"I'm great on advice." Scully laughed and slapped Dolly's fat thigh. "I don't know about the information. Ain't that right, Dolly?"

"Oh, yes," she agreed. "You're great on advice."

"All right, Sheriff, what do you want to know?"

I sat down and filled and lighted my pipe, thinking how much the situation had changed since last Sunday when I had come into this same tent loaded for bear. What really shocked me was the knowledge that in my thinking and planning I'd come to rely on Ben Scully, a man I might have had a gunfight with before now.

"You know what happened a week ago Saturday night when I arrested two of your men and shot Morgan," I said. "This made Rip Yager so mad he could spit nickels. He cussed me for chasing some of his business away. He said men wouldn't come to town Saturday nights if they expected to get shot and what we needed was a professional star toter."

Scully and Morgan laughed. Morgan said: "I wish to hell you had been a professional. I wouldn't have this foot hurting like it is."

Scully nodded. "Yager's a fool. What he don't know is that you did something a professional probably wouldn't have done. You bulled your way into it headfirst and risked your fool neck, but you got away with it. You made yourself a reputation and it will pay off. You didn't have any trouble last night, did you?"

"Nothing of importance," I said, "but Yager doesn't want the camp run that tight. Likewise Doc Jenner, Bailey, and Steele all

83

feel the same way, so they've decided to send for a professional."

"I suppose a professional wouldn't run as tight a camp as you will," Scully said. "Who'd they send for?"

"Captain John Wallace."

Scully had been adding a column of figures and half listening at the same time. Now he laid his pen down and placed both hands on the top of his desk and stared at me.

Ten-Sleep Morgan said in a low, incredulous tone: "My God."

Scully didn't say a word for a long time. He just sat there without moving a muscle, but his face wasn't the pokerface I had thought it was. I couldn't believe it, but the man was scared. Not the ordinary fear, the kind we all feel on occasions, but a panicky fear that makes a man tuck his tail and run like hell. I simply could not understand it. Ben Scully was a number of things, but being a coward was not one of them.

Then Scully took a handkerchief out of his coat pocket and wiped his face. He slipped the handkerchief back into his pocket and yelled at me: "Why in the name of all that's holy did you let them do it?"

I yelled back: "I didn't! They never told me what they were going to do. Yager sent for me and told me he had asked Wallace to come to Angel's Landing. The other three had agreed."

"I suppose they want you to deputize Wallace."

"That's right," I said, "and I told them I wouldn't do it."

"Well, that's to your credit," Scully said.

He took a long cigar from his pocket, bit off the end, and lighted it, taking his time. Finally he asked: "Why did you come to me, Sheriff? I can't give you any information or advice that will do you any good."

"Yes, you can," I said. "All I know about Wallace is hearsay. I figured as much as you'd been around, you'd know something about him personally."

"Something?" Scully laughed shortly. "I know a whole hell of a lot about him, but I ain't sure you want to hear it."

"Try me," I said.

He nodded. "All right, I will. I never started a business in a camp that Wallace was ramrodding, but in three camps I've had the bad luck of having some fool like your friend Yager send for Wallace."

Scully jabbed a forefinger at me. "I'll tell you what kind of a man Wallace is, or was when I knew him, and I doubt that he's changed. In every one of those three camps the men who brought him there were sorry they had, and then they had one hell of a time getting rid of him."

"Why was that?" I asked.

"I'll tell you why," he said bitterly. "He's the one man on this green earth that I'm afraid of, and I've met a lot of hardcases. The reason I'm afraid of John Wallace is that he's the only man I know who will kill another man for no good reason."

Scully hesitated, then went on. "I mean, no good reason the way you and I see it. There are no rules to the game he plays. He kills men because they're in his way or to scare the living hell out of people in a camp when he gets there." He jabbed a forefinger at me again. "I'll lay you ten to one that the first night he works in Angel's Landing he will kill a man."

I looked at Ben Scully and tried to swallow, but I couldn't. I thought: *It will put it up to me if he does that here.* "How fast is he?" I asked.

Ten-Sleep Morgan and Scully exchanged glances, then Morgan said: "He's the fastest man I ever saw and I've seen them all. He's older now, and he may have slowed up, but in his prime I don't think Hickock or Earp or any of them could have matched him."

"A lot of fast men will use every bullet in their guns to hit anything," I said. "A slower man who's accurate can probably take them."

Morgan shook his head. "Not Wallace. He'll shake five slugs out of his iron and place them all within six inches of each other in your brisket." Morgan shook his head again. "No, Girard, he's a killing son-of-a-bitch. I figure I've got more than an average man's guts, but I walked away one time from a gunfight with Wallace. I never did that before or since, and I guess I'm ashamed of it, but then I know I wouldn't be alive if I'd fought him."

"You see," Scully said, "when he goes into a mining camp or a cow town, he levies a tax on every businessman in that camp or cow town. The money goes into his pocket. He'll bring along a few plug-uglies who don't admit they know him, and he won't admit he knows them, so you can't prove anything on Wallace or his men, but the funny thing is that the businessman who doesn't pay the tax gets beaten up or has his place robbed or it burns down." Scully spread his hands. "So it doesn't take long for everybody to find out that the smart thing is to pay."

I couldn't believe the situation would be as bad as they were claiming, but on the other hand they were hard-headed businessmen who didn't scare easily, so I couldn't discount what they said.

"What are you going to do?" I asked.

"Sell out," Scully said quickly, "if I can find a buyer. I won't put up that building I was talking about. I've been in this business too long to risk my neck in a camp that might not last. When's he coming?"

"Rip didn't say," I said, and this time, when I looked at Scully's tight-featured face, I knew the situation would be fully as bad as he and Morgan had said.

"What are you going to do, Sheriff?" Scully asked.

"I don't know," I answered, "but I won't let him come in here and start killing people for no reason."

"That's what I thought you'd say," Scully said. "Now I'll give it to you straight. You've got two choices. Resign or let Wallace have the camp."

"I won't do either," I said. "I've got a third choice."

"That makes you a dead man," Scully said.

Morgan nodded somberly. "You're dead and you're beginning to stink."

I walked out of the tent, leaving enough gloom behind me to turn the day dark. I didn't feel any better myself. I had never been one to worry about anything before it happened, but I figured that if men like Scully and Morgan were boogery about Wallace's coming, then I had plenty of reason to be boogery, too. I'd be a fool if I didn't, but I'd always been convinced that there was a solution to any problem if a man could see it.

I had a terrible feeling that I'd been lucky all my life, but that fate had finally made the wrong shake of the dice for me. If there was a solution to this problem, I sure as hell couldn't see it.

CHAPTER THIRTEEN

For the second time that afternoon I turned around before I reached my house. This time I went back to Yager's Bar. I'd thought of something I needed to ask Rip. I found him sitting at a poker table, a half-filled whiskey bottle on the table in front of him. He was a little drunk, but not so drunk he couldn't think or talk straight.

He looked at me, his lips curling sourly under his white mustache. He said: "You come back to apologize for being so damned stinking about Wallace? Maybe you started remembering how we helped raise you from the time you was small enough to be crawdad bait."

"No, Rip," I said, sitting down across the table from him. "I thought you'd want to apologize."

"Me?" He sounded surprised. "I ain't got nothing to apologize for. All me and the others was trying to do was to protect Angel's Landing."

There was no point in arguing with Yager, but I couldn't keep from saying: "What you're really trying to tell me is that you insulted me and Ralston when you claimed we couldn't do the job of protecting Angel's Landing. We've done it so far, Rip. I figure we can go on doing it."

He sighed and for a moment I thought he was going to cry. He said: "Mark, we sure didn't aim to insult you and Tug. I told you before and I'll tell you again that it's just a case of neither one of you having the experience you need."

"I'd understand that if you'd sent for anybody else but Captain John Wallace," I said.

I shut up, though there was plenty I wanted to say. I just sat there, looking at the old man, and then I began to feel sorry for him. He was so damned anxious to get all the business he could. So were the others, now that the opportunity had been dropped into their laps.

Maybe Rip was honest in what he'd done; maybe I'd made a judgment about him I had no right to make. I was sore and I was hurt, and maybe that was the reason I had condemned him the way I had. Honest or not, he'd made one hell of a mistake, but he'd gone too far to back down.

He stared at me, not saying a word for a time. The corners of his mouth were still quivering. Finally he said: "We figured we was doing you a favor, getting you and Tug out of a tough job."

Again he might have been honest in saying that. I knew very well that none of us had wanted this to happen, at least at first. Maybe they did now. I had accused them of wanting to fill their own pockets and none of them had really denied it, but I might have been wrong in condemning all of them.

I started thinking about it in a little different light then, now that I was here with Rip Yager who had been a good friend through the years when I'd been growing up. I realized that my feelings had been governed by the fact that my old friends did not have any confidence in me, and that had hurt more than I had realized.

"All right, Rip," I said. "What I came back for was to ask you how you could pretend that Wallace has any authority to serve as a marshal if I don't deputize him?"

"I wish you didn't feel the way you do about deputizing him," Yager said, "but we thought you might, so we wrote to the county commissioners, telling them what we were doing and why we were doing it. They're authorizing Wallace's appointment as a special officer to serve in Angel's Landing during the time of emergency, the length of the emergency to be decided by the four of us who asked Wallace to come."

"That's not legal," I said. "I'm the only man in Bremer County who can do that."

"Maybe it ain't legal," Yager said, "but by the time you or anybody else can take it to the Supreme Court, the state of emergency will be over and you and Tug can run things any damn' way you want to."

I rose, knowing he was right about that. Anyhow, Wallace was the kind who would serve without even a hint of legal authority. I asked: "When is he getting here?"

"He'll come to Durango on the train Friday afternoon," Yager said. "He'll stay there that night and come to Angel's Landing Saturday in time to handle the job that night. Meanwhile I'm letting everybody know about him. I figure that will get rid of most of the scum that's moved in on us."

I turned toward the door.

Yager called: "Mark, what are you going to do?"

I stopped and looked back. "I don't know, Rip. I honestly don't know."

This time I did go back to the house. I smelled the good smell of cooking food the instant I stepped through the front door. I called: "What's going on in here?"

"It's your good fairy," Abbie answered from the kitchen. "It's about time you got here. This fairy is getting mighty hungry."

I went into the kitchen and found Abbie standing beside the stove wearing a white apron decorated by a red band and equally red embroidery across the bottom. She had a dab of flour on her nose, the way a good cook should have; she was hot and her cheeks were flushed; and in that moment she seemed to me the loveliest woman in the world. Suddenly she became very important to me.

I walked to her and hugged her and kissed her, and her arms came up around my neck as she kissed me back. When I let her go, I said: "I couldn't have told you what love was when I asked you to marry me, but I do now. Let's get married. I mean, in about two weeks."

She patted my cheeks and stared at me intently for several seconds. "Something's happened," she said. "Tell me about it."

I'd heard about women's intuition, of having second sight, of being able to read men's minds, but I had not believed it. I did now.

"Why, it just looks as if Tug and I are off the hook," I said. "Yager and the other old-timers have asked Captain John Wallace to come here to serve as town marshal. Of course we don't have a town, but we pretend we do."

She was very sharp, sharper than I had thought she was. She knew what Wallace was. Not as much as I did, of course, but she knew his reputation. She said: "I see. What does that make you and Tug?"

"Oh, we supervise the rest of the county," I said casually.

But she wasn't to be put off. She said: "Yager and the others don't believe you can take care of your job. Is that it?"

"That's about it," I agreed.

"What are you going to do?"

"I don't know yet," I answered, "but I do know I'm not going to turn the town over to Wallace."

She motioned to the table. "Sit down. I've still got to make the gravy."

I sat down and filled and lighted my pipe. I hadn't told her that Scully and Morgan had said I was a dead man and I didn't intend to, but I underestimated her again. She brought the food to the table and ate in silence.

The notion of being a walking dead man sent prickles up and down my back. It was an idea I just couldn't get used to. Maybe

I refused to accept it, although logically I didn't know what I could do to stay alive.

When we finished eating, Abbie said: "I've been the one who didn't want to wait, but you've kept putting it off. What changed your mind?"

"I've told you why I didn't want to get married now," I said. "I didn't want to leave you pregnant and have you struggle to raise our child the way my mother struggled to raise me, but I've been thinking about it. I'm going to make a will in the morning and leave everything to you. You couldn't run the stable, but with the camp booming like it is, you could sell for a good figure. Put that money with what's in the bank and you would be taken care of for a while. After the child got older, you could go back to teaching."

"I agree to all of that," Abbie said, "and I'd be happy to get married this minute if we could, but I think there's more to it than that."

"I guess there is," I said. "I've thought about dying the last few days more than I did before and I can't bear the thought of dying before we have each other."

I had been looking at her, but I lowered my gaze, a new thought coming to me, a thought that must have been in my mind without my becoming fully conscious of it. I said: "All of a sudden it seems important to me to leave an heir. Maybe that's the immortality the preachers talk about."

She rose and came around the table to me. "Oh, honey," she said softly as she put an arm around me. "I want you to have an heir and maybe you're right about it being immortality, but I can't accept the idea that you're going to die now. What put it into your head? You've never talked this way before."

"Oh, I don't know," I said. "It's just that when you're enforcing the law, you risk your life whenever you walk down the street."

"I'm way ahead of you," she said. "I've thought of all of this before. It's why I've been ding-donging at you to get married. I want to have your baby, but you're doing a complete turn-around. It's Wallace's coming, isn't it?"

I hadn't intended to tell her this much, but there didn't seem to be any use to deny it. I nodded. "Yeah, it's Wallace. He's coming to Durango on Friday. He'll be here on Saturday. I feel like I'm forking a bad horse. I can't stay on and I'll break my neck if I get off."

"Then let's get married tomorrow," she said.

"I'll see the preacher in the morning," I said.

I wasn't as happy as a bridegroom should be, mostly because my mind wouldn't leave Wallace. The only way to handle a man like that was to shoot him in the back. That was where I ran into a stone wall. I couldn't do it to save my life or to save Angel's Landing from a reign of terror.

The whole thing seemed crazy. Here was a man who had no moral scruples whatever, a man who could murder me without thinking twice, a monster any way you looked at him. He deserved no more consideration than a mad dog, which in fact he was.

Regardless of this, I could not murder him in cold blood because of my moral scruples. Even if I did, the town would have my hide. I'd get strung up because I'd be reversing the picture and making myself the monster and Wallace the victim, and that was no answer to my problem.

CHAPTER FOURTEEN

As it turned out, we had no wedding that day. During all the time I had lived in Angel's Landing, we'd never had a preacher—I mean a resident preacher who regularly held church. We did have itinerant preachers who traveled through the country and stopped and held service in the schoolhouse or Yager's Bar, then went on to any of the dozens of little mining camps scattered throughout the San Juans.

If we had a real need for a preacher, a wedding or a funeral, we sent to Durango for one or went to Durango, which was usually the easiest and cheapest thing to do. Or, on a few occasions when we were faced with a death and the family could not afford to get a Durango preacher, Doc Jenner had served and had done a commendable job. Actually we'd had few such emergencies because we'd had few funerals and fewer weddings.

It would be different now because a preacher named William Manning had moved to Angel's Landing a week ago. He was living with his family in a tent with a sign in front: *ANGEL'S LANDING COMMUNITY CHURCH*. He'd held Sunday service in the schoolhouse and had announced in the Angel's Landing *Weekly Gazette* that he intended to stay and build a church house.

I had met him and had not been impressed, but then I have seldom been impressed by a preacher. In any case, I thought he'd be glad to marry us, and he could do the job whether he was impressive or not. I went to his tent first thing Monday morning, but he wasn't in sight.

The day had started as one of those cold damp mornings that we get in the mountains quite often during the summer. The rain hadn't amounted to much more than a mist dropping out of a weepy sky, but there had been enough moisture to make your clothes cling to you and bring out the rheumatism in old people. And, of course, enough to make wood that was stored outside too damp to burn well.

Mrs. Manning was having her troubles. She was squatting beside a smoldering fire in front of her tent, trying to cook breakfast. Half a dozen kids were hunkered around her, all of them whimpering or complaining about being hungry.

I guess this was the reason I had never been impressed by preachers. This Manning was typical of the ones we had seen in Angel's Landing. If they were single men and wanted to starve, that was their privilege, but to drag families around and fail to support them was criminal. In my opinion, they ought to go to work, but I swallowed my irritation and asked for the preacher.

Mrs. Manning stood up and wiped the rain off her face. I guess she knew me or had had me pointed out to her. She said: "He's not here, Sheriff. His mother in Denver had a stroke and he left yesterday afternoon to go to Durango to catch the train." She swallowed and wiped her face again, then added: "He took every cent we had to buy a train ticket to Denver."

The kids were huddled around her, staring at me, wide-eyed. They had stopped whimpering. I noticed they were clean, good-looking children. Mrs. Manning was about thirty and pretty in a fragile sort of way, like a wildflower that had been plucked and was beginning to wilt.

"I'm sorry," I said. "I'll see him later."

"He'll be gone all week," she said. "Maybe longer if he can't borrow money to come back on the train. It'll take him a long time to walk that far. I'll have to conduct the services till he gets back." She hesitated, then asked: "Is there anything I can do? Any message I can give him?"

"No," I said. "My business can wait."

I was never one to give money away, but this was a tragic situation and I knew I'd be seeing these hungry kids all day in my mind. I dug a gold piece out of my pants pocket and placed it in her hand. I said: "Go to the hotel and get a good meal for your children, Missus Manning. When we get a day like this, it may stay damp till evening, so don't try to nurse that fire any longer."

She looked at the coin, and then at me, and I had never seen a more thankful expression on a human face in my life than I did in hers. "Thank you, Sheriff," she said. "Thank you very much."

"You're sure welcome," I said, and walked away fast. She had started to cry and I felt like joining her as I thought of a few remarks I'd like to make to her husband when he got back.

When I reached my house, I saw Abbie coming around it from the garden. She saw me and waited until I reached her, then she said: "I was going to do some weeding and thinning today, but it must have rained harder during the night. The ground is so muddy I'll have to wait a day or so."

I stood there, looking at her, feeling sore and disappointed and frustrated. I wanted her, I loved her, and I could not understand what had happened to me. Or her. I wasn't sure which, but the odd thing about it was that I had known Abbie for several years and had always considered her pretty ordinary as far as beauty went, but now, wearing an old dress and with her hair and face damp with the rain, she was beautiful.

I told her so, blurting the words out and then getting as red-faced as a schoolboy. She was pleased and came close to me and kissed me. "It's wonderful what the miracle of love can do to a man's vision," she said, "and I don't care who sees me kiss you. I guess I'm the happiest woman in Colorado. Is this our wedding day?"

"No," I said, "and I'm disappointed. The preacher went to Denver and he'll be gone for a week. I'd say for us to go to Durango, but I don't think I ought to leave."

"No, you can't leave," she said. She glanced at the house and back to me, and added softly: "I'm tempted, Mark. I'm sorely tempted."

"So am I," I said.

We stood looking at each other, and it made me feel good to know she was wanting me as much as I wanted her, but I wasn't one to push her into anything against her will. In the end her sense of propriety was too much.

"I guess we can wait a week, Mark," she said.

"I guess so," I said, "but I don't want to."

She patted me on the cheek. "Neither do I."

"I'm going to see a lawyer," I said. "The will can't wait. I should have taken care of it last week."

She gripped my arms, her eyes wide and frightened. "Mark, you've found out something."

I shook my head. "No, I don't think there will be any trouble until Wallace gets here."

"And after that?"

I still didn't want to tell her all that I knew or had heard, and I certainly didn't want to tell her about my fears, which were considerable. So I said: "We'll just have to wait and find out, but I'm going to see a lawyer right now. Since I don't have any living kin that I know of, it would be a mess if I fell over dead from a heart attack."

I left her standing there beside my house, her face mirroring her concern. I couldn't help wondering what she would have said if I'd told her I was more worried about a dose of hot lead than I was of a heart attack.

Two lawyers had moved into town during the past week. One was using a tent for an office and proclaimed in his sign that he was an expert on mining laws. That was no concern of mine, so I went to the second one, a young man named Jerry Carruthers who had rented a cabin next to the bank and had spent the last few days cleaning it up.

When I stepped inside, Carruthers was sitting at his desk trying to look busy. The room was spic-and-span, the smell of paint hit me the moment I went through the door, and an impressive row of law books was on the wall behind him. I shook hands, telling him who I was.

Carruthers nodded, saying: "I know who you are, Sheriff. The newcomers spot you right off, but I guess it will take some time for you to get acquainted with us."

"That's right," I said. "Angel's Landing is not what it used to be." I motioned toward Main Street, which was filled with loaded ore wagons headed for Durango and empty ones returning to Banjo Creek, freight outfits, and a conglomeration of rigs, men on foot, and others on horseback.

"They say history repeats itself," I said. "It sure has here. When I was a kid, I remember Main Street looking just the way it does now except that we didn't have the ore wagons then."

"Well, what can I do for you?" he asked.

"I want you to draw up my will," I said.

He was surprised and showed it. "I want the business and I'm not trying to discourage you, but you're a young man and you look healthy."

"I am right now," I said. "I want to leave everything to Miss Abbie Trevor." I spelled both names for him, then added: "I have no living relatives that I know of, and, if any turn up after my death, I don't want them to have my money. Miss Trevor and I plan to be married in a few days."

"We can fix it legally, of course," he said, still puzzled, "but I'm curious why you don't wait until you're married. You'll have to have another will drawn up then, and, if that is to take place in a few days, why not wait?"

"Because I may not be alive then," I said.

This set him back a little. He leaned forward, his eyes searching my face. "Sheriff, I'm getting outside of what is really my business, and I apologize, but damn it, I just don't understand why a man of your age and health is worried about the next few days."

I was irritated, and I guess I showed it, but I thought that what was going to happen in Angel's Landing was his business as well as mine, so I said: "Some of my friends who have been in business here for years do not think I can handle the law enforcement problems that we're going to have, so they've sent for Captain John Wallace to serve as town marshal. I expect trouble with Wallace."

He leaned back in his chair and groaned. "I guess almost everybody in the West has heard of Wallace. Why would they send for him? He'll make trouble for all of us."

"I don't really know, unless they haven't heard what I've heard," I said, "but they seem to think there will be anarchy in Angel's Landing if I'm left in charge, and it will make them lose business. They don't want anything to happen here like it did in Creede when Soapy Smith was running the camp. They think that hiring Wallace will scare the riff-raff out of town."

"It will scare some of the rest of us, too," he said bitterly. "I hear he's a killer if you cross him, so I sure as hell won't risk it."

"But I can't keep from it," I said.

He got up and walked to a window, and for a moment stood looking out at the traffic on Main Street, then he said reluctantly: "I'm not a gunman, Sheriff, but the men who want Wallace don't know what they're getting. If I can help when the time comes, I'll do what I can."

I was surprised. I looked at Carruthers for a moment, think-ing he couldn't do one damned bit of good, but he was willing. I said: "I'll remember that." I wondered how many other men in town would say the same thing. Or, if they did say it, how many would actually put their lives on the line when the time came?

"I've lived in some pretty damned lawless towns, and I know that I won't get any legal business if it happens here, but Wallace law isn't the answer." He returned to his desk and sat down. "I'll have the will finished by four o'clock this afternoon, God willing, so you can stop and pick it up then. We'll have to have it witnessed."

"I'll be here with witnesses," I said, "but it may be after four."

"I'll be here till six," he said, and laughed wryly. "You never know . . . some more business might wander in from the street."

I left his office and made my rounds of the town, thinking that there was more pounding and sawing than usual, more traffic on Main Street, and more strangers in town. All of this was to be expected, and I figured there would continue to be additional growth for weeks, maybe months.

Then I reached Ben Scully's big tent and I began to wonder if I was wrong to expect more growth. The front flaps of the tent were tied down, and a big sign pinned to the front of the tent said: *CLOSED.*

Chapter Fifteen

I stood there a couple of minutes, staring at the sign. It didn't quite add up, Scully's going off and leaving his tent here. If he hadn't gone off, why had he closed his business? It was a big tent and must have cost a good deal of money. I knew he'd bought two lots from Doc Jenner, the one the tent was on and the lot beside it, the one on which he'd intended to build.

Scully had said he was going to sell out. I figured he meant the lots because he'd surely take his tents and gambling equipment and furniture to use in some other camp. I walked around to the back and saw that the small tents were gone. The back flap was up, and, when I heard voices from inside, I decided he was still there.

I walked into the tent, but Scully and Morgan weren't in sight. Two men were playing cards, the gambling equipment, the bar, and the tables and chairs had not been moved. The men glanced up and grinned.

"Howdy, Sheriff," one of them said. "Ben said you'd be around."

They were familiar, but it took me a moment to place them, then I recognized Redbeard and Baldy, the two men Tug and I had jailed the first Saturday night.

"Howdy," I said. "I thought you two buckos had left camp."

"We've been prospecting up the creek," Baldy said, "but, hell, it's staked out all the way to the head of the cañon, so when Ben offered us this job, we took it."

Redbeard nodded agreement. "If you ain't been up the cañon lately, you'd be surprised what's going on. They hit another vein way up on the other side of the Lucky Cat. Before they're done, they'll have a dozen working mines all the way up Banjo Cañon. Not high-grade ore like Dolan got out of the Lucky Cat, but ore that's worth sending to Durango."

Baldy nodded. "It'll be a good camp and it'll be here for a while. Of course it'll be hell trying to carry on a business with John Wallace running things."

I guessed that they'd been working for Ben Scully all the time, but I didn't push it. I also guessed that they were hoorahing me, but I didn't push that, either. I asked: "Where's Scully?"

"Him and Ten-Sleep went to Durango," Baldy said. "He's selling out. I thought he told you."

I nodded. "I thought he meant his lots."

"He thinks he's got a buyer for the whole kit and caboodle," Redbeard said. "He's talking about going to Alaska. If he does, he'll buy what he needs in Seattle before he leaves the States."

"We're just keeping an eye on things for him," Baldy added. "If the new buyer won't give us jobs, we'll go to Alaska with him."

I walked out of the tent, thinking that if Ben Scully knew as much about Wallace as he did, then others would know, too, so why would anyone else come to Angel's Landing to buck Wallace if Scully didn't want to?

I spent the morning patrolling Main Street, not because I felt that it was absolutely necessary, but because I wanted to be seen and to think about what was happening.

New businesses had sprung up since dawn, most of them in tents, although a few shacks had been thrown up at both ends of Main Street. One man was working the old shell game. He shot me a worried glance every time I walked past him, but he kept making pitches.

Farther up the street a big sign had gone up in front of a tent saying that Professor Harold J. Hollingsworth was a phrenologist and would give you a complete analysis of your personality. A huge picture of a man's skull decorated one side of the sign. It was marked off into various sections, each of which was supposed to control certain gifts such as imagination, artistic ability, musical talent, and the like.

Beyond that tent was another that housed a Gypsy fortune-teller named Madam Zorah who could foretell your future. To me they were all con games, but, as far as I knew, these people were not breaking any laws.

If the men on the street were suckers enough to spend their money on the elusive pea or getting the bumps on their heads felt or listening to Madam Zorah tell their future, it was their business. One thing I had learned was the simple fact that I could not keep people from committing acts of stupidity if they chose to do so.

The only problem I had all morning concerned a miner who woke up with a head as big as a dishpan. He'd gone to sleep with a whore in her tent, but when he woke up, he was lying in the sun, his pockets empty.

He pointed out the woman's tent. When I lifted the flap and stepped inside, I found her asleep. The morning was hot and in the tent it felt like a furnace. She was partly under a blanket, and, as far as I could tell, she was completely naked. I suppose that during the cool part of the night she had pulled the blanket over her, but now that it had turned hot, she had thrown it back so it only covered her legs.

I guess I woke her when I stepped into the tent. She grabbed the blanket, pulled it up over her, and started cursing me with one of the best vocabularies I ever heard.

"You're under arrest for theft," I said. "Get your clothes on. The jail's empty, so there's no reason why you can't have a cell all to yourself."

She was middle-aged, too fat, her hair frowzy, and the sweat that ran down her cheeks and chin had spread her paint over her face in a crazy-quilt pattern. Suddenly she was very modest, trying to wrap the blanket around her so she was entirely covered except for her face.

"You want me to get up and dress right here in front of you!" she screamed. "If you think you're going to get to see . . . !"

"It wouldn't be any great pleasure, ma'am," I said. "I've seen prettier female bodies when I was a working cowboy, especially when I was behind 'em."

She glared at me, so furious she could not say a word for a few seconds, then she said, tight-lipped: "You ain't putting me in your lousy jail."

"That's up to you," I said, "but, if you don't want to do what I'm going to suggest, I'll take you down Main Street to the jail just the way you are. I reckon you won't get cold on a day like this, though you may get a sunburn. Rolling a drunk is one thing I won't stand for. It's bad enough taking his money for sleeping with him. I can't see that it was any bargain."

She started cursing me again, then stopped and chewed on her lower lip as if suddenly realizing she was digging her grave a little deeper. Finally she asked: "What do you want me to do?"

"Give the man his money and get out of town," I said. "There's a stage leaving for Durango in about an hour."

She didn't take long to make up her mind. She yanked a purse out from under her pillow and threw it at me. "Get to hell out of here while I dress, you bastard!" she screamed. "I ain't giving you no free show!"

"It would have to be free, ma'am," I said. "It sure wouldn't be worth paying for."

I left the tent. When I came by on my next round after returning the money, she was gone. It was noon, so I stepped into the hotel dining room for dinner. Joe Steele was at the desk in the lobby, but he ignored me as I walked past him.

It was a sorry situation, I thought. Here was a man I'd known all these years, a man I had thought of as my friend, a man who in a way had helped raise me, as Rip Yager had said, now acting as if he didn't know me from any of the hundreds of strangers in town.

After I'd eaten and paid for my dinner, I stopped at the desk. "Remember me, Joe?" I asked. "I'm Mark Girard. I didn't think you'd forget me after eighteen years."

"I ain't likely to forget you," he grated. "We did what we thought was right for you as well as the rest of us, and we ain't getting one damn' bit of co-operation. We figured to help you stay alive, but a lot of thanks we're getting for it."

"You've got all the law and order you want, haven't you?" I asked. "That's what you wanted, wasn't it? You didn't want anarchy, you said. Well, you haven't got it."

He swiped a hand across his face. "You and your god-damned pride. You can't keep us from having anarchy or some con man from running the camp and you know it. One's as bad as the other. The real crowd ain't got here yet. It'll be hell on high red wheels when it does come. You ain't figgered that out yet."

"I'd keep the lid on all right if I had the proper help," I shot back. "If I don't get it, me and Tug will do it by ourselves, not John Wallace, unless he murders us."

I wheeled and walked out, too angry to continue the conversation. Sure, I knew I was being stubborn, but the way I saw it I didn't have any choice. As far as being murdered was concerned, I had no doubt Wallace would try. I had wanted Joe Steele to think about it. Steele and the others could still stop Wallace from coming, but as I pushed through the crowd to the livery stable, I knew they wouldn't.

Suddenly I knew what I was going to do. I don't know why

an old truth popped into my mind just then, but the idea that when trouble is coming, you'd best get the jump on it made a lot of sense. I'd be in Durango Friday when Captain John Wallace arrived.

CHAPTER SIXTEEN

When I reached the livery stable, Dutch Henry told me that he'd rented every horse and rig we had and I ought to buy a dozen more horses. I'd better take advantage of the business before I had any competition, he said, but I told him I didn't have the capital to go in that deep. I was going to Durango on Friday, though, and I'd bring back two more horses.

He gave me a sharp glance, then said: "John Wallace gets into Durango on Friday, don't he?"

"So you've heard," I said.

He nodded. "It's all over town. Rip Yager wanted folks to know, I guess."

"I've had my will made today," I said. "As soon as Tug gets back, I want you two to go with me to witness it."

"Now wait a minute . . . ," he began, then stopped and took a long breath. "Who the hell knows what'll happen when that bastard gets here? There's an old Dutch proverb that says a man should always step on the head of a snake before the snake gets his teeth into a man's hide. I guess that's the way you figure it."

"That's about the size of it."

"Tug will have to stay here on Friday, I reckon," he said. "There's got to be at least one lawman in town, so maybe I ought to go with you to Durango to help fetch them horses back."

"No, I'll manage," I said, "but thanks for offering to help."

"I'm a fair hand with a gun," he said.

"Maybe later," I said. "I don't expect to settle anything in Durango, but I want to lay the cards out face up so he can see them."

He nodded. "Good idea. If you need me later, just holler. I was a deputy once, you know, before I caught the gold fever. It was a long time ago."

I didn't know, but it made me feel good that an old man like Dutch Henry would offer to help. Nobody else had except Carruthers.

I spent the afternoon in the jail office getting caught up with some paperwork, then returned to the stable to wait for Tug. When he arrived a few minutes later, I told the boy to take care of Tug's horse and then asked Tug to go with Dutch Henry and me to sign the will.

He didn't ask any questions just then, but walked with us to Carruthers's office. The lawyer had the will ready. We signed, I paid him, and we left.

"Come over to the jail office," I said. "I've got some things I want to go over with you."

Tug still didn't say anything until we settled down, then he asked: "What's all this about a will, Mark? Ain't you feeling good?"

"A little puny," I said.

I told him about Wallace's coming and that I was going to Durango to see him. Tug sat, staring at the ceiling for a long time, his hands clasped behind his head. Finally he said: "This is one hell of a note and no mistake. I knew old Rip was getting boogery, but I didn't figure on anything like this."

He got up and paced around the room for a while, then said: "Maybe we ought to do what Yager and the others say, just stay out of town and let Wallace take over."

"We can't do that," I said, more sharply than I'd intended to.

"You know what it would mean. I don't think we can entirely stop him, but we've got to let him know we're here."

"Sure, the normal risks that any lawman takes," he said sourly. "Well, I can see why you want your will made, not being married yet to Abbie, but damn it, Mark, I am married and I've got a baby and I can't afford to get killed."

"You knew the risks when you took the star," I said.

"Sure, the normal risks that any lawman takes," he said, "but not the certainty of getting killed. I've never seen John Wallace, but I've heard the stories about him just like you have." He sat down in his chair again. "Mark, Yager and the others must have heard the same stories, too, so why did they send for him?"

I told him what Joe Steele had said about helping me stay alive. I added: "Those men have been like four fathers to me. I didn't believe Joe when he said that, but maybe it is part of the answer. It's possible they expect us to back off and let Wallace do the job here, then get rid of Wallace, and you 'n' me would still be alive and the camp would be curried down so we wouldn't have any trouble."

"Maybe," he said, as if he didn't believe a word of it. "I think it's more likely a proposition of them simply not figuring we can handle the type of toughs who drift into a camp like this and we'll give the town a bad name and that'll hurt their businesses."

"Well," I said, "Wallace will keep the lid on, all right. He'll kill anybody who tries to pry it off."

"Where they're making their big mistake is thinking they can get rid of him," Tug said.

I nodded. "The second mistake is thinking he'll fix it so more business will come to Angel's Landing. Nobody's going to invest in a town that's run by a madman."

"It was before my time," Tug said, "but I guess that Wallace was the right kind of lawman to ramrod a town in the early days. The trouble is he operates just like he used to. Rip and the others are living in the past."

"Well, let's get back to your problem," I said. "You can resign Saturday as soon as I get back. I'll pay you for the part of the month you've worked."

He grinned a little. It wasn't much of a grin because he wasn't in a humorous mood. "I'd like to quit, Mark. By God, I'd sure like to, and right now I'm sorry as hell I ever took this damned star, but I ain't a man who can walk out, neither. I guess I want to show that cussed Doc Jenner that we can be good lawmen as well as good cowboys."

"I figure we can," I said. "I'm not sure how, but I've got a hunch Wallace can be handled. That's the reason I'm going to see him in Durango. I'm not willing to admit I'm dead yet. There's got to be a way."

I didn't sleep much that night. I lay there in the darkness staring at the ceiling, a faint ray of moonlight coming in through my bedroom windows. I ran the situation through my mind time after time, and, when the sun came up, I still had no idea how to take care of Wallace.

If I tried to arrest him after he had killed his first man, and that was something he would probably do Saturday night, he'd call me into the street. If I tried to draw, I'd be dead before my gun was clear of leather.

It would be stupid to start practicing now and hope to become a fast-draw wizard by Saturday. I was a good shot with a six-shooter, but I had never been fast getting my gun out of the holster and firing. I had watched men who were both fast and accurate. I had tried to imitate them, but I simply did not have the co-ordination or rhythm or whatever it is that goes into making a man fast on the draw.

When I agreed to run for sheriff, it had never occurred to me that I would have to face a situation that demanded a fast draw. I thought, as Tug had said, that those days were gone, but John Wallace still lived in those days and he would bring them with him to Angel's Landing.

I got up, shaved, and ate breakfast, but I didn't feel as if I had slept any during the night. I supposed I had, but it had been a restless sleep, so I might just as well have stayed up. I stepped out of the house into the hot morning sunshine. I looked at the timbered ridges bordering Banjo Creek and I thought: *This is a damned beautiful world. I'm not ready to leave it.*

As I walked to my office, I told myself I might be leaving this world in a few days. I still had no idea how I would handle Wallace when the time came. I thought that maybe he wouldn't be as bad as we had heard, maybe he had changed with the times.

I remembered the old saw about most of the things we worry about never come to pass. Nothing helped. I had a feeling in my guts that he hadn't changed, that he was as bad or worse than we had heard, and, if I didn't stop him, nobody else would.

When I reached the office, I saw that Tug was still asleep on his cot, so I didn't bother him. I had forgotten that the Angel's Landing *Weekly Gazette* was printed on Monday nights and distributed on Tuesday mornings. The editor and publisher, Alexander Miller, had showed up in camp two weeks ago with his press, had rented a shack about a block down the street from my stable, and then had set out to sell ads in his newspaper.

The first issue hadn't won any prizes in journalism. Most of what he had printed was stock stuff that I suppose he had stolen from a Durango paper. He had a few ads and a typical article on the mines in Banjo Cañon, the high-grade ore that Catgut Dolan had showed us, and some hyperbole about the future of Angel's Landing as a mining and commercial center.

Someone, and I never did find out who although I suspected
Rip Yager, had left the second issue on my desk. It was folded
so I couldn't see the headlines, but when I opened the paper
and saw them, they hit me like a blow in the belly.

*CAPTAIN JOHN WALLACE
TO SERVE AS TOWN MARSHAL*

Below, in smaller print, were three more lines:

*ALL LAWLESS MEN ARE WARNED TO LEAVE TOWN
THE LAW WILL BE ENFORCED TO THE LETTER
REIGN OF TERROR WILL BE ENDED*

I glanced at the first paragraph which read: *A local committee
of established businessmen headed by Rip Yager, owner of Yager's Bar,
informs your editor that the famous lawman, Captain John Wallace,
has been hired to serve this community as marshal. He will arrive
Saturday next to assume the marshal's position immediately. Captain
Wallace has served with distinction in such lawless towns as Dodge
City, Leadville, and Miles City.*

I slammed out of the office and headed for Miller's print
shop. I didn't take time to count ten. I was so damned mad I
was out of my head. All I could think of was that the *Gazette*
was saying that Angel's Landing was filled with lawless men,
that we were suffering a reign of terror, and therefore it had
been necessary to hire Wallace.

The front door of the print shop was locked. I stepped back
and hit it with my shoulder—the flimsy lock broke, the door
snapped open, and I lunged inside. No one was around, but I
knew that Miller had a kitchen and bedroom in the back, so I
rushed on through the maze of paper, press, composing table,
and assorted junk to the back room.

No windows were open and even at this early hour the room

was stifling. Miller was asleep. I jerked the blankets off the bed and hauled him to his feet. He was wearing a long flannel nightgown. How he could sleep in a hot room with two blankets over him and wearing a flannel nightgown was beyond me.

He let out a scared yelp, then I shook him till his teeth rattled. I slammed him back on the bed and shouted at him: "Tell me who the lawless men in town are, Miller! Who is it that's warned to leave and when hasn't the law been enforced? What reign of terror have we been having?"

Alexander Miller was a small and inoffensive man. He lay frozen, his eyes wide, slobber running down his chin. I dropped my right hand to the butt of my gun. When he saw me do that, he screamed: "My God, Sheriff, don't kill me!"

"You're not worth the powder," I said. "Who told you to publish those lies?"

"Rip Yager," he quavered. "He figures that the toughs will leave town as soon as they know Wallace is coming."

I wasn't sure who the toughs were, now that Ben Scully and Ten-Sleep Morgan had left town. I should have expected this. As Dutch Henry had said, Yager wanted everyone to know that Wallace was coming. He hadn't been satisfied to let the news get around town by word of mouth. It had to be in the newspaper so the outside world would know, too.

It was the line about the reign of terror that curried my hide. I said: "Miller, there has been no reign of terror in Angel's Landing, and you know it. You'll have a retraction in the next issue or I'll beat the living hell right out of you."

"Yes, sir," he whispered. "You'll have it."

I walked out then, but I didn't feel any better. The damage had been done.

CHAPTER SEVENTEEN

I was drinking a cup of coffee in my office and Tug was eating breakfast on Thursday morning when Ben Scully's man—the one I called Redbeard—walked in. He said: "Howdy." I nodded at him. He was grinning as if he knew something I didn't. That irritated me. My nerves had been tight enough all week to serve as fiddle strings.

"What the hell's eating on you, mister?" I asked.

"Well, Sheriff," he said, "I'm just a messenger. I was to ask you to come to Ben's tent. There's somebody who wants to meet you."

I wasn't in any mood to go gallivanting off to meet somebody who could walk over here as well as I could go there, so I said: "He can get over here if he wants to see me."

Redbeard shrugged and made a kind of a snickering sound. "It's up to you, Sheriff, but she sure will be disappointed." He wheeled and strode out.

Tug looked up from his plate. "Did he say *she?*"

I put my coffee cup down. "That's what I thought I heard."

"Well, you'd better go see who that *she* is," Tug said, grinning. "I won't tell Abbie."

I got up. "I will if you don't," I said. "I guess I had better go see, now that I'm curious."

I left the office, not having the slightest idea who had sent for me. The front of the tent looked just the way it had all week. I walked around to the back and found that one of the small tents had been put back up.

Stepping inside, I saw a woman sitting at one of the tables. She was dressed in a bright red velvet gown that came clear to the floor when she stood up. She was too fat, but she was a big woman, so the fat wasn't as evident as it would have been on a smaller one. She wore her hair in curls as a young woman might have done, but it looked out of place on her. She wore too much paint, and she'd put on some perfume that hit me when I was still ten feet from her.

She smiled as she rose. "You're Mark Girard, aren't you? You're the little boy I fed pie and cake to a long time ago, aren't you? Only you're not a little boy any more." She shook her head as her gaze ran up and down my body. "It's hard to believe."

Maggie Martin! I guess my mouth dropped open from sheer surprise. I don't think I'd thought of her since before the flood. I certainly hadn't expected her to show up in Angel's Landing, and, now that I was actually seeing her, she didn't look much like the Maggie Martin I remembered.

She came to me while I stood there as if I had grown roots into the ground. She put her arms around me and just sort of enveloped me. For a moment I thought I was being smothered. About the time I stopped breathing, she backed up and looked at me.

"Well, Mark, you've grown up into a fine, big man," she said. "I've thought about you so often and I've wondered what happened to you. I remember how some of my girls kept telling me I'd get all of us into trouble and make your ma mad. Did she ever find out?"

I shook my head. "She never did."

"And now you're sheriff." She took my hand and led me to the table where she had been sitting. "Do you want a drink?"

"No thanks."

She sat down and motioned to a chair. Redbeard and Baldy

were sitting at another table, both of them grinning as if they were a whole lot smarter than I was. Right then I had a hunch that they were.

"Now tell me about yourself, Mark," she said after I sat down. "What have you done and where have you been and what are you going to do?"

"Oh, I've been as far away as Durango," I said, figuring I might as well make my life experience as ridiculous as possible. I had no idea what she was after, but I was dead sure she was after something or she wouldn't have sent for me. "I grew up here and took care of my mother till she died. I'm going to be married next week. I own the livery stable. That's the total of my biography."

She kept on smiling, playing the part of a pleasant and easy-going woman. She said: "You haven't had a very adventurous life, have you?"

"No, ma'am, I haven't," I said, "but I liked my life real fine until Catgut Dolan made his strike on Banjo Creek and turned the world upside down."

"That's what he done, all right," she agreed. "And now you've got some problems, haven't you?"

I nodded. "Ben Scully called me a clodhopper sheriff and I guess he's right."

She laughed aloud and slapped a fat thigh. "From what Red tells me, you do your job."

"He ain't as much clodhopper as Ben made out," Redbeard said. "We spent a night in two of his lousy cells."

"That makes you a little more than a clodhopper, Mark," she said. "These men are tough customers. I've known them for a long time. It takes a good man to handle them."

"I aim to do the job they elected me to do," I said.

"I'm betting that you will," she said. "I've been around a good deal since I had the Pleasure Palace here in Angel's Landing when you were a boy. I've been in Deadwood and Leadville and Miles City. I've had some nice places and I've been pretty lucky and I'm going to try it here again. I bought Ben Scully out."

I let on I was surprised, though I wasn't really. I'd had a hunch that was what had happened and why she had sent for me, but I played it cozy and said I was glad she was here and hoped she would have good business.

"I'm sure I will," she said. "I've never built the kind of layout that I really want. I've dreamed about it and drawn up dozens of plans, but I never hit just the right camp where I thought I'd stay. Now maybe I'm making a mistake, but I think Angel's Landing will be a good business camp for years. What do you think?"

"From what I hear about the new strikes they're making up Banjo Creek, it will be," I said.

She leaned toward me. Her face, which had held a mask of good nature, now turned tough and hard. She said: "I hear that John Wallace is coming to Angel's Landing. What are you going to do about him, Mark?"

"I don't know," I answered.

"Well, by God, you'd better know," she said. "I've been driven out of two towns by that bastard because I couldn't pay the tariff he was collecting. He ruined those towns and broke almost every businessman there. He didn't leave until he had their money. He'll do the same thing here."

"If he breaks the law, I'll arrest him," I said.

She laughed. It wasn't a good sound, one of contempt rather than humor.

"Listen, boy," she said, and she made the word *boy* sound as if I was still the kid she had given pie and cake to, "I got this outfit cheap from Ben Scully because he didn't have the guts to fight Wallace again. He's lost out in other camps, too. Just like I

117

have. Now I aim to build a place here that you and everybody else will be proud of, an honest place where a man can get a woman, a drink, or a game, and know that he's getting his money's worth. Well, I want to be protected, or I'll walk out the same as Ben Scully did."

I rose, irritated and insulted. "Don't call me *boy*, ma'am," I said. "I told you I'd arrest him if he broke the law, and I will."

I started to turn around to walk out, but she came up out of her chair fast for a fat woman and grabbed my arm. "I'm sorry, Mark, but this is important to me. It's the chance I've been looking for as long as I've been in business. I've got a right to know what you're going to do to keep Wallace from cleaning this camp out just like he has the other ones that hired him."

"This is the third time I've told you," I said angrily. "If he breaks the law, I'll arrest him."

"Oh, my God." She threw up her hands. "Don't you know that nobody arrests Captain John Wallace? Nobody can draw a gun as fast as he can. Nobody operates without any conscience the way he does. Nobody can scare the living hell right out of you by looking at you the way he can. Now what makes you think you can arrest a bastard like that?"

"I can try," I said. "It's all you can expect of any man."

"And you'll get killed," she said. "That's what I don't want to happen. If you're gone, there's no one left to fight. He'll have his own way for sure."

"There's got to be a way," I said. "I haven't thought of it yet, but I will. I'm going to Durango in the morning. I aim to talk to him. Maybe I can convince him he shouldn't come to Angel's Landing."

"He'll kill you before he even gets here!" she cried. "Listen, you idiot. All that it takes when you're talking to him is to make a move with your right hand. You're going after your pipe or a pocket knife or a bandanna to blow your nose and he'll draw

118

and kill you and say you were going for your gun, and everybody who's watching will testify you might have been doing just what he said. He's supposed to be a lawman, so no one questions him very much. It'll be murder, Mark. Just plain murder."

I looked at Redbeard and Baldy, who weren't acting as smart as they had been a few minutes before. I would get no help from them. Then I looked at the woman. I could see the greed in her, but she had a right to the protection she was asking for.

How was I going to give it to her? I still didn't know, so I didn't have anything to tell her. I just walked out, and this time she let me go.

CHAPTER EIGHTEEN

Abbie cooked supper for me that evening. Afterward she cleaned up the kitchen while I sat at the table and smoked. When she finished, we went out to the back porch and sat down. The evening was warm enough to be comfortable, so we stayed there a long time while the day turned to dusk, and then night came with its millions of stars and the hills bordering Banjo Creek became black curves against the lighter sky.

I wasn't sure how much Abbie knew about John Wallace. I had not told her all that I'd heard and I didn't tell her about Maggie Martin's being back in town. I didn't tell her I was going to see Wallace in Durango on Friday, either. I thought the less she knew the better, but I think she sensed what was happening and what lay ahead for me.

I didn't say it in words and neither did she, but there was a strange feeling between us that evening, as if we didn't want it to end because it might be the last time we'd be together. At least that thought was in my mind and I had a hunch it was in hers.

Later we walked to her house with our arms around each other. When we reached her gate, she asked: "You'll be back Saturday?"

"I sure will," I said. "I'll buy the horses tomorrow and leave Durango early Saturday."

She didn't say anything for a moment. She just stood there with her head tipped back, trying to see my face in the darkness, then she raised a hand to my face and ran her fingertips over it. Suddenly she began to cry and hugged me with a fierceness I had not felt from her before.

"Hey, what's the matter?" I asked.

"Oh, Mark, you know what's the matter!" she cried.

She brought my face down to hers and kissed me, then whirled away and ran up the path to her house. I walked back slowly, convinced that she did indeed know, but whether from woman's intuition or from hearing the gossip was something I couldn't decide.

The week had been the longest of my life, and it wasn't over yet. The night dragged on second by second. Sometimes I would drop off for a few minutes, and then I'd be awake again. I tried to imagine what John Wallace looked like. He must have horns and a tail, I thought. I had yet to hear anyone who had known him in recent years say anything good about him.

I had a good look at death that night, too. Not that I could understand it, or know what happened to a man when he died. I thought about what a good world it was, or had been for me anyhow, about my mother, about my father, who must have lived a frustrating life, and then I thought about Abbie and how much I loved her and wanted to sleep with her and wanted her to have my babies.

I tried to think of some way I could meet Wallace and shoot it out with him and have a chance to survive. Some trick, a hidden gun, a knife, words I could use to talk him out of wanting to kill me, or to leave Angel's Landing as soon as he got here, or not to come at all.

Finally the dawn light began seeping into my bedroom, and I had no more idea what to do than I'd had when I'd gone to bed. I was damned scared. That was all I was sure of.

I got up, dressed, had breakfast, and shaved, then walked to the livery stable through the cool, wine-like air of the high country. As I saddled my horse, Dutch Henry came dragging along the runway, rubbing his eyes and yawning.

"You're getting away early," he said.

"It's a long ride. I want to buy my horses today so I can leave early tomorrow morning. I figure I'll have a tough day tomorrow."

"You're aiming to see Wallace today, ain't you?"

"I'll try to," I answered. "There's a six o'clock train. I'll meet it just on the chance that he'll be on it."

He peered at me in the dim light, then said: "I don't know why you're so hell-bent on committing suicide, Mark. It strikes me that you'd be smart to wait till he gets here. You've got lots of friends in Angel's Landing. I don't think you've got that many in Durango."

"Yeah, I have got lots of friends here, all right," I said, and mounted and rode out through the archway.

I didn't want to tell him because I would have hurt his feelings, but the friends I had in Angel's Landing including Dutch Henry wouldn't be any help when it came to fighting John Wallace, and I couldn't see any other end to this.

Sooner or later Wallace would step over the thin line between what a lawman could do and could not do, and I would have to go after him. It would be Mark Girard against John Wallace any way I cut it, and friends wouldn't do me one damned bit of good.

I glanced along the street and saw Rip Yager come through the batwings and throw a bucket of dirty water into the street. Rip had a lifelong habit of waking at dawn regardless of the season, the weather, or what he had to do that day. During all the years he had run his place alone, he had come to the saloon by sunup and had swamped it out. He was still doing it from habit, I guess, though he had enough hired help so he could have stayed in bed.

I reined over to him, calling: "Good morning, Rip."

He stood looking at me, ramrod straight, an old man who refused to accept his age. He still felt he could make a fortune out of his saloon, that there was a lot of life left for him, and he aimed to live it, and that was probably the reason he had done what he had.

He was sore at me because I aimed to stop Wallace. Maybe he was honestly afraid I'd get killed. On the other hand, maybe he thought I might succeed. I wasn't sure any more how he felt about anything.

Anyhow Rip's—"Good morning."—was as frosty as a January freeze.

"I'm going to Durango to buy a couple of horses," I said. "Dutch Henry says I need a dozen, but I can't afford that many. While I'm in Durango, I'll see Wallace. I'm going to try to persuade him not to come to Angel's Landing."

"He'll come."

"I'll make it clear to him that he will have no authority as a sheriff's deputy, and he will not be allowed to use the county jail. He will also receive no pay from the county. He might change his mind."

"He won't." Rip's eyes narrowed, and for an instant I thought he felt some concern for my safety. He said: "Don't provoke him, Mark."

"I guess you know what kind of man he is," I said, "or you wouldn't say that."

"I know he's handy with a gun and I know he has a short temper," Yager said. "I just want you to stay out of his way until he's chased all the riff-raff out of camp, and then we'll send him away and you and Tug can go back to what you're doing now."

I lost my patience then, and I said sharply: "Damn it, Rip, there isn't any riff-raff in camp."

"We'll have 'em," he said. "It won't be long."

123

"Rip, don't you know what his record is in other places that have hired him?"

Yager shrugged. "Lies."

"No they're not," I said. "I talked to Ben Scully before he left. I've talked to Maggie Martin. They both have been in towns that hired him. He's a leech, Rip. He gets a pay-off from every business in town. You pay or you get your head knocked off. He'll bleed the camp white."

"I wouldn't believe anything a whore like Maggie Martin says." Yager started to turn toward the batwings, then paused to add: "Ben Scully is the riff-raff I was talking about. I'm glad he's gone." He waggled a finger at me. "He left because Wallace is coming, not because of anything you or Tug did."

He went on into the saloon then, ending the conversation. I reined back into the street and headed south for Durango. Yager and the others had gone too far to back down. They'd learn the hard way, I told myself bitterly, and then they'd come to me for help, help which I didn't know how to give them.

As I rode, I told myself that Wallace was only one man. He pulled his pants on one leg at a time like any of us. He couldn't do everything that it had been said he'd done, and that, of course, was exactly the way Yager and his friends looked at it. But, damn it, he had done the things I'd been told about, and not alone, either. He had toughs who did his muscle work for him, and the chances were I'd never be able to prove his connection with the plug-uglies. That was his strength.

What could I prove if I took him before Judge Manders? I had given some thought to looking up the judge after I got to Durango, but had discarded the idea. There was nothing he could tell me at this point. The court was helpless until a crime had been committed, and, after it was committed, I'd still have to have witnesses, providing, of course, that I was still alive. If Wallace was alive, I probably couldn't get anyone to testify against him.

I stabled my horse as soon as I arrived in Durango, had dinner, and then looked up the trader I usually dealt with. It took the balance of the afternoon, a good deal of riding to check out the two animals, and some haggling before I bought the horses for a figure that I considered reasonable.

It was almost 6:00 P.M. when I finished. I ran to the depot that was four blocks away. The train had just pulled in and had stopped with the squealing of brakes and jangling of the bell, and it was still puffing like a huge, prehistoric monster.

I walked along the line of cars, trying to see a man who could be John Wallace. I didn't know what he looked like, but it was easy to check off the passengers by the simple process of elimination. None fitted.

I turned back, disappointed, and decided to try the hotels. I took a room in the first one I came to, about a block from the depot. I asked: "Has John Wallace registered here?"

"Captain John Wallace is registered here," the clerk said, emphasizing the word *Captain.* "He and his wife arrived on the two o'clock. They're in room One-Oh-Four just across the hall from you. They'll be leaving for Angel's Landing in the morning. He rented a horse and buggy for the trip he told me."

"Thanks," I said, and crossed the lobby to sit down in one of the chairs that lined the wall along with the geraniums.

I could go up to his room, I thought, but I decided I wanted to look at him before I jumped him. I was surprised that he had a wife, but it wouldn't make any difference. She might as well hear what I had to say, so I settled down to wait, certain that I would know him when I saw him.

CHAPTER NINETEEN

I guess I waited fifteen or twenty minutes, studying every person who walked through the lobby. Most of them were single men, largely drummers who were heading for the bar or moving from the dining room to the bar. A few were miners and several were cowboys. I judged the only couples to be ranch people, probably in Durango for an overnight visit to buy supplies.

Then I saw them. I didn't have the slightest doubt about their identity from the minute they came down the stairs. The woman was younger than I expected, actually a girl hardly out of her teens. She was very pretty, and I could see why Wallace or any man would be attracted to her.

As they walked past me and moved to the dining room, I watched them, particularly the girl's hind end, which swayed with a titillating rhythm. This was something that a woman learned; it was too exaggerated to be natural. A woman had only one reason to learn to walk that way, and I will admit I made a judgment about Mrs. Wallace that was far from complimentary.

Wallace looked to be about the right age, somewhere in his middle fifties. He wasn't a big man, but he contrived to look bigger than he was. I had seen other men who could do that, men who considered themselves very important and wanted to impress everyone who saw them.

It has always struck me as a weakness because a man who is really important never has to do anything to convince other people that he is. I'm not really sure how Wallace managed this unless it was the way he held his shoulders and kept his back overly straight.

The main thing that gave the man away was the way in which he carried his pearl-handled .45, very low and tied down in the manner of an old-fashioned, professional gunman. Now few men carried guns unless they were lawmen, and no one carried his gun in that manner. At least I had never seen it done before, though I had heard about it from old-timers like Rip Yager.

This bore out what I had suspected, that John Wallace was a relic from the dead past, a fact that did not make him any less dangerous because to him the past was not dead. He lived as though this was still the 1870s, and he would force me to live the same way.

I had thought through exactly what I was going to do. I waited until I was sure they were seated at a table, then I rose and crossed the lobby to the dining room door. I paused there until I saw them, then threaded my way through the maze of tables to them.

Not waiting for an invitation to sit down, I pulled a chair back and dropped into it. I said: "You're John Wallace, aren't you?"

He glanced up from his menu, only then aware of my presence. "Captain John Wallace, sir," he said, his voice reflecting his annoyance at my intrusion.

I could see Mrs. Wallace on my left, but I kept my eyes pinned on her husband as I placed my hands, palms down, on the top of the table. I said: "I'm Mark Girard, sheriff of Bremer County. Notice that my hands are in sight. When I leave, I will clasp them back of my head. If you shoot me, it will have to be accepted as murder because it will be evident to all of these witnesses that I have not made any kind of motion toward my gun."

Wallace was speechless. He sat there, staring at me for what must have been a full minute. I used that minute to get a good look at him, and I guess one fact struck me harder than anything else. Captain John Wallace did not have horns and a tail. He was a man, no more and no less. Here I was, chills chasing each other up and down my spine as I sat a few feet from a man who had been in my thoughts for days, a man who had terrorized me and had certainly terrorized Ben Scully and Maggie Martin.

The simple truth was that there wasn't very much about Wallace that was different from me or anyone else. He was a handsome man, deeply tanned, with a strong chin and a full-lipped mouth. He had brown hair with just a touch of gray at the temples.

The only feature that set him apart from anyone else was his eyes. They scared me. I had never seen eyes like them. I have heard it said that a man's eyes are the windows of his soul, and, if it was true, I'd have to say that John Wallace had no soul.

The eyes were the lightest of blue, so light that they seemed nearly colorless. More than that, they held no expression whatever. They might have been the eyes of a dead fish, and I could believe that he was capable of killing a man without feeling a shred of remorse.

As this thought came to me, I had a strong urge to get up and leave the dining room. I hoped I didn't show that temptation on my face, although I knew my breath had quickened and I had a feeling I was almost panting.

"Well, I'll be god damned," Wallace said softly. "I will tell you something, Girard. I have no intention of shooting you. Not here anyhow. What happens in Angel's Landing is another matter."

"Perhaps you are thinking that it will wait till we are in Angel's Landing," I said. "That's why I'm here. I'm asking you not to come to Angel's Landing."

"I'll have to say no to that request," he shot back. "I have a contract with four men including Rip Yager, who, I understand, is the unofficial mayor of the town."

"No more than anyone else," I said. "It just happens that he is the oldest settler and in the past, when Angel's Landing was practically dead, he liked to call himself mayor the same way that some of the rest of us called ourselves the town fathers. That doesn't apply now. The camp has changed."

"I understand that," Wallace said. "That's why I've been hired."

"There's no need for you to come," I said. "Yager talks about lawlessness and riff-raff. There is neither. The town is not incorporated. The only unit of government below the state is the county. I'm the sheriff of that county. I have handled and I will continue to handle all problems of law and order. You will have no authority to act as a law officer. You will therefore be outside the law, and, if you create any problems, I'll arrest you."

He looked at his wife and laughed. "Ain't this the damnedest thing, Garnet? Yes, sir, it purely is."

She laughed, too, a little nervously, I thought. I glanced at her, realizing she was not as young as I had first thought. She said: "Yes, John. It certainly is."

I brought my eyes back to Wallace's face immediately, but I had observed that she was a blonde, her hair more gold than yellow, and that her eyes were bright blue. She had a red-lipped mouth and trim, firm breasts that were lifting and dropping rapidly, and she was breathing fast. I wondered if she was as scared as I was.

"I don't need any of your damned authority to come to Angel's Landing," Wallace said evenly. "I make my own laws in a camp like that, and it's pretty plain to see that you've got a good thing going or you wouldn't try to keep me out. I think, Girard, that the melon is big enough for us to split."

I knew what he meant, all right, but I let it go because I didn't want to get sidetracked or to force the issue. I said: "Listen and you listen damn' good because I want every card turned face up on the table. You will not receive one nickel of pay from the sheriff's office. You will be denied the use of the county jail. I will see to it personally that you don't bleed the town white as you have other places where you have served as marshal. The only pay you'll get will be what Yager, Steele, Doc Jenner, and Bailey give you, and that will not be enough to satisfy a man of your appetite."

He had been astonished at first, I guess, or maybe stunned, but I could see now that his temper was boiling. Not from his eyes, which were as expressionless as ever, but from the rosy glow of his cheeks and the twitch at the corners of his mouth.

"You've had your say," he said. "Now I'll have mine. I don't need anything from the sheriff's office. My authority will be given me by the county commissioners. I don't need your jail. I will, beginning tomorrow evening, ramrod the camp, and I advise you to stay out of my way."

"And if I don't?"

"Then I shall surely kill you. I have made an agreement. I will carry it out to the letter. As for arresting me, mister, that's the wildest dream I ever heard. Nobody arrests Captain John Wallace. Nobody."

And that, I remembered, was exactly what Maggie Martin had said to me. "One more thing," I said. "I'm going to ask Yager to meet with you and me and the other three in his back room as soon as you show up tomorrow. I want all of them to hear what I've just said to you. I don't think the county commissioners have the legal right to appoint you any kind of a law officer, and I want that on the record."

"If you don't ask Yager for that meeting, I will," Wallace snapped.

I stood up, my hands clasped back of my head. I turned, glancing again at Mrs. Wallace, who had an amused half smile on her lips, and left the dining room. As soon as I was out of Wallace's sight, I lowered my hands, got my bandanna out of my pocket, and wiped my face. My shirt was wet and sticking to my back. I strode out of the hotel into the cooler air of the street and took a long breath.

I walked west, found a restaurant, and went inside. I ordered a meal, but I couldn't eat after the food came. It stuck in my throat. I knew I didn't want to risk seeing Wallace again, not until I was back in Angel's Landing.

Maybe he didn't have horns and a tail, but I was satisfied that he was the genuine, fourteen-carat, murdering son-of-a-bitch that Scully and Maggie had said he was, and that he'd kill me without the slightest provocation if he saw a way to do it without making trouble for himself.

I did not go back to the hotel to sleep in the room I had rented. Instead, I slept in the livery stable where I had left my horse. I rode out of Durango at dawn with the two animals I had bought.

CHAPTER TWENTY

When I reached Angel's Landing, I went first to the livery stable and turned the two horses I had bought in Durango over to Dutch Henry. He looked at me questioningly. I nodded and said: "Wallace got there. He'll be here sometime this afternoon."

I walked to Abbie's house from the stable to tell her I was back. She wasn't there, but a moment later I found her on her knees in the garden back of my house, weeding a row of radishes.

She wanted to know what had happened, and I told her briefly, adding: "I don't suppose I did any good. I sure didn't talk him into not coming, but I guess I didn't really expect to."

"What are you going to do now?" she asked.

"I don't know. I'll have to see what he does."

Tug Ralston was waiting in the jail office for me. He said: "We had a quiet night here. How was it in Durango?"

I told him what I'd done. He asked me the same question Abbie had, and I gave him the same answer I'd given her.

He paced back and forth in front of my desk, pulling on a cigar. He said: "It's been too damned quiet. I suppose the news that Wallace is coming has scared some of the rowdies out of town."

"Maybe," I said.

"There is one thing," Tug said. "A big man rode into town yesterday, a hell of a big man. He must stand half a foot taller than me, and I'll bet he weighs two hundred and fifty pounds. No fat on him, neither. He calls hisself Shell. No first name.

Just Shell. This morning he rode up Banjo Creek."

I looked at Tug, figuring there was something more. I said: "Well, I guess there's no crime riding into town whether you're a big man or a small one."

"Maybe not," Tug said, "except that last night he called on some small places, saloons mostly, telling 'em that they'd be smart to pay ten dollars a week for protection against broken windows, robbery, fire, and so on. Anything you want to name. I guess they all paid except Maggie Martin. She told him to get out. This morning she's got about ten slashes in the side of her tent. Looks like somebody just ripped the canvas with a knife."

"So it's starting," I said, "and Wallace isn't even here yet."

"You figure there's some connection?"

"Sure there is," I answered. "It's my guess that Wallace will promise to stop it, but he's going to have to be paid."

Tug nodded. "We'll never prove the connection."

"Maybe not," I said. "I want you to be with me at Yager's Bar when Wallace gets here. We'll see what he says about this man, Shell."

Yager just grunted when I told him I wanted to meet with Wallace and the other three men who had brought him here.

"Won't do no good," he said. "You'll just kick up some dust. Damn it, Mark, give Wallace a chance."

"Oh, he'll have his chance, all right," I said, "but I figure to kick up some dust. You heard about a man named Shell?"

"I heard," Yager said. "I don't like it no more'n you do. That's the first thing Wallace is gonna have to work on."

I saw Steele, Doc Jenner, and Bailey, and all of them agreed to be in Yager's Bar by the middle of the afternoon. I was there ahead of them with Tug. They all strolled in about 3:00, acting casual as if this was a very ordinary occasion.

Wallace didn't show up until almost 4:00. I was standing in

133

front of the saloon when I saw him pull up in his buggy at Steele's hotel. He got out, gave his wife a hand, and carried two big suitcases inside, then drove away to my livery stable.

I started toward the hotel, hoping to reach Wallace to tell him we were waiting for him, but there was so much traffic on the boardwalk that he got away before I could reach him. I stepped into the lobby and found Mrs. Wallace, waiting beside the suitcases.

I said: "Remember me, Mark Girard? We met last night."

She carried a pink parasol. Now she fiddled with it nervously as she nodded. "I remember you, all right. You put John into one hell of an ugly mood."

She glanced toward the door, then lifted the parasol and placed it across her right shoulder as if she didn't know what to do with it. She was more nervous than ever, her face unsmiling and showing lines of strain that had not been there last night. Again I sensed that she was older than I had first thought and certainly older than she wanted people to think she was.

"Tell your husband we're waiting for him in Yager's Bar," I said. "It's down the street half a block or so."

"I'll tell him." She glanced at the door again, then leaned forward as she moved the parasol from her shoulder, and tapped the tip against the floor. She said in a tone so low I barely heard her: "I've got to see you, Sheriff. Alone. Where do you live?"

I told her, but I didn't like the smell of it. I said: "Can't I see you here?"

"No, no," she said quickly. "John must not know about it. He'll be busy most of the night. He won't come to bed until almost dawn. I'll be at your place about midnight."

I nodded and turned away, still not liking it at all. I sensed a trap, but I figured that as long as I recognized it, I could keep from falling into it. I returned to Yager's Bar, thinking about Mrs. Wallace. I couldn't shake the feeling that somehow she aimed to deliver me into her husband's hands.

There was something about the woman that didn't add up, but I couldn't put my finger on it. I sensed that Wallace completely dominated her, but I couldn't tell whether she resented it or not. Maybe he was her meal ticket.

Some women put up with a hell of a lot just to get their three squares a day and a roof over their heads, but Garnet Wallace wouldn't have to. She had the looks and figure to choose her own meal ticket. I remembered then that I had not seen a wedding ring on her hand and I wondered if there was some significance to that.

Wallace got there in another fifteen minutes. The saloon was crowded with miners and cowboys and drummers and the usual hangers-on that any saloon has, but he didn't waste any time. The instant the batwings slapped shut behind him, he yelled: "Yager! Rip Yager! You in here?"

"Here!" Yager called. "Right here, Mister Wallace."

"Captain Wallace," he said.

"Yes, sir," Yager said as he held out his hand. "Welcome to Angel's Landing."

Wallace ignored the extended hand. He said: "I believe we're supposed to have a meeting, or so your cowboy sheriff said. Let's get at it."

"Yes, sir," Yager said, dropping his hand. "Back here."

In that brief exchange I saw two things that amazed me. One was the way Yager simply collapsed and turned into an old man in a matter of seconds. He was shaky and pale, and he seemed to totter uncertainly as he led Wallace across the saloon to the back room. He was scared, I told myself, more scared than he would admit. I had a hunch he'd been sorry for quite a while that he'd sent for Wallace, but his pride had kept him from backing down, and now it was too late.

The second thing was the huge star that Wallace wore on his

vest. It was at least twice the size of the star I carried. There was no sense in having one of that size, but he did have it, and it was big and shiny. Sterling silver, I thought, to glitter the way it did. No one would ever call it a tin star. It was a symbol of the kind of lawman Wallace pretended to be, of course, and I had a hunch it was effective.

I said to Tug in a low tone: "Keep your hands away from your gun."

He nodded, understanding. We followed Doc Jenner into the back room. The others were ahead of us. Yager closed the door. Before he could say a word, Wallace said brusquely: "Your cowboy sheriff called this meeting. If he hadn't, I would have. I wanted to know who you are. Let's hear your names."

Doc Jenner, Steele, and Bailey introduced themselves. Wallace made no effort to shake hands and he pointedly ignored Tug who stood beside me.

"You understand . . . ," Yager began.

Wallace held up his hand. "I'll do the talking, Yager. You sent for me to keep law and order in this camp and I propose to do exactly that. Your cowboy sheriff tells me I will receive no salary from the county, so I expect the people of this camp to raise the money to pay me, and that starts with you men who sent for me.

"Your cowboy sheriff also tells me I will be refused the use of the county jail. Gentlemen, that is no hardship. I won't need a jail. I will warn a man once, and then I'll kill him if he continues breaking the law. If a man starts to draw on me, I will kill him. It doesn't take much of that to make a camp shape up. Now just stay out of my way." He strode to the door.

I said: "Wallace. . . ."

He wheeled to face me. His eyes seemed paler than ever. He said: "Captain Wallace."

"Wallace," I said, "you are not living in the Eighteen Seven-

136

ties. You start killing men like you're talking about and you'll see the county jail from the inside."

He stared at me, his eyes narrowing, his right hand close to the butt of his gun. I was holding the buckle of my belt tightly with both hands, and I was very careful not to make a move of any kind.

"Step outside, Sheriff," he said. "We'll settle right now who is going to be the law in this town."

"No," I said. "It would be suicide."

"You're right about that," he said, "but it leaves you a coward, and no man who is known as a coward can enforce the law. You will be out of town or dead within forty-eight hours. That is a promise."

He left the room. None of us said a word until he had threaded his way through the crowd in the saloon and disappeared into the street. Then Joe Steele said softly: "I'll be damned."

"I'll be god-damned," Joe Steele said. "I guess the stories are true about that bastard."

Rip Yager sat down and wiped his face with his bandanna. He said: "You were right, Mark. What do we do now?"

No one answered.

CHAPTER TWENTY-ONE

I could think of a number of adjectives that would fit John Wallace. At best he was a madman to have talked the way he did about not needing the county jail because he would warn a man once about breaking the law, and, if he did it again, he would kill him. I had never heard anyone talk that casually about taking a human life, and it proved to me at least that he was a mad-dog killer and should be treated accordingly.

Now Wallace was searching for a man he could kill. I was as sure of that as I had ever been sure of anything in my life, but I had no idea how to stop him. I think the same thought was in the mind of every man in Yager's back room.

Doc Jenner was the only man to put it into words. He said: "Mark, I'm sorry. We should have listened to you. I guess I was as responsible as anyone for bringing Wallace here. This is the moment of truth and there's no way to dodge it.

"I saw a chance to make a lot of money out of the lots I bought years ago when they were dirt cheap, and I panicked because I was afraid someone like Soapy Smith would get control of the town and no one would want to invest here. Now we've got someone worse than Soapy Smith. As long as he's here, no one will want to invest."

"I don't see what you want us to do," Tug said sourly. "If we try to arrest him, he'll simply pull his gun faster and kill us."

"Can't you tackle him from both sides at the same time?" Bailey asked.

"Which one of us do you pick to die?" I demanded. "It might be both of us. From what I hear, he's fast enough to take both of us. Anyhow, whichever one of us told him he was being arrested would be dead."

"Mark could deputize one of you to help," Tug said.

He was being ornery, but I didn't blame him. I almost laughed when he said that because it was downright comical to see all four men shake their heads and start backing off. It was working out exactly as I had known it would. Once these men who had brought Wallace to Angel's Landing realized what the situation was, they would look to us for help and we still didn't know how to give it.

"He'll be on you men for more money than you've contracted to pay him," I said, "and he'll be on every businessman in town. The women, too. A lot of them will leave like Ben Scully did. I don't mind telling you that Tug and I are pretty damned sore about it because you didn't trust us to do the job we had been doing and could go on doing. If you had been willing to give me the money you've promised Wallace, we could have hired a couple more men."

"We plead guilty," Yager said somberly, "but there's got to be a way to get the drop on that kill-crazy bastard."

"I've been trying to think of it," I said. "I'm still thinking. Come on, Tug. We might just as well find out what Wallace is up to."

We left the back room and bucked our way through the crowded saloon to the street. The instant we cleared the front door I saw that something was happening, but it took me a moment to see what it was. About half a block down the street the traffic had cleared away. Even people on the boardwalk had ducked into stores and the hotel lobby and offices.

Wallace was standing in the middle of the street. Facing him, about ten feet away from him, was a cowboy I had seen in town

139

a few times. His name was Whiskey Bowman. He worked for the Rafter B, a big spread south of Paul Kerr's place. He came to town three or four times a year just to turn his wolf loose.

I'd never had any problem with Bowman, though I knew he was a bully and plenty of other men had had trouble with him. It was just that he'd never gone on a real tear since I'd started packing the star.

I was too far from the men to hear what was being said, but I could see that Bowman was drunk and mean and was giving Wallace a cursing. Wallace had found his man to kill. Bowman was too drunk to know what was happening, or maybe he didn't even know who Wallace was. I started toward them, but I was too late. Wallace took one step forward and said something, and Bowman went for his gun.

I had seen men draw, mostly in saloons where they were showing off, or on the 4th of July when there was a lot of shooting going on and the cowboys who were in town were carrying guns and trying to out lie each other, but I had never seen a man pull a gun with the cold-blooded purpose of killing someone else. I was seeing it now, but I still found it hard to believe.

I had the weird feeling that Wallace's gun jumped out of his holster into his right hand. It didn't, of course, but his hand moved so fast that it gave that impression. Wallace fired three times before Bowman's hand touched the butt of his gun.

The three shots pounded into each other and rolled along the street in what seemed one giant explosion of sound, then the echoes came and died. Bowman was in the dust, not moving, and Wallace was standing over him, his smoking Colt in his hand.

I ran toward them, Tug a step behind me. Men began to edge out of doorways, not sure yet that they wanted to be in the street. I reached Bowman and knelt beside him. He was dead. I was sure he would be, but I was shocked to see that the three bullet holes in his chest were close together and any one of them would have killed the man.

Wallace looked at me, a small, contemptuous smile on his lips, his big star reflecting the light of the afternoon sun. He asked: "You want me for murder, Sheriff? Or do you call it justifiable homicide?"

I told myself I still didn't want to commit suicide, and that was what I would do if I tried to arrest Wallace. Besides, there was no doubt about what had happened. Bowman had gone for his gun. I don't know how Wallace had done it, but somehow he had goaded Bowman into drawing.

"Self-defense," I heard myself saying. "That makes it justifiable homicide."

Men had formed a circle around us. Doc Jenner examined Bowman and ordered one of the men in the circle to go for the stretcher in his office. Wallace glanced around the circle, his face expressionless, his gun still in his hand.

"I want you men to know that I'm the law in Angel's Landing," he said. "The sheriff is a coward as you all saw. He has forfeited any right he or his deputy has to claim to be the law in this camp."

What he had said was calculated to force me into drawing my gun. It didn't work, but it brought closer the moment when I would have to make my play, or he would be proved right in saying I had forfeited the right to claim to be the law. I faced him, my right hand hanging motionlessly at my side.

"You're a little early to be talking about who's a coward and who's the law," I said. "I'm still sheriff."

I turned and walked away, my cheeks burning. Tug strode beside me, saying: "I knew Bowman. He wasn't much of a man, but he shouldn't have been trigger bait for that bastard."

We started toward the jail, then I changed my mind. I said:

"Let's go see Maggie Martin."

Tug nodded. He said: "We ain't got much time, Mark. That son-of-a-bitch set this up just the way he wanted it. Now it's our play."

"Mine," I said.

"Ours," he snapped. "This is what I signed on for. You ain't leaving me out. Don't try."

I didn't answer. I saw no use to argue, but I knew there was nothing Tug could do. Somehow this had to be handled between me and John Wallace. I looked up at the blue sky and thought I had never seen it so beautiful. I thought of Abbie and told myself I couldn't die now, not with the whole world giving me all I could possibly want. No, I couldn't die at the hands of a man like John Wallace, who should have been destroyed a long time ago.

We found Maggie sitting in a rocking chair in front of a small tent that was directly behind her big one. She nodded somberly at us. She said: "I can guess what happened down the street, but tell me."

I told her, then asked: "Is that the way he always starts?"

"That's the way," she answered. "He guns somebody down. It doesn't make much difference who it is. One killing sets him up. After that, he gets what he wants because nobody will face him. Usually the regular lawman, if there is one, resigns and leaves town. Is that what you're going to do, Mark?"

"No," I said.

"Then you'll be dead in forty-eight hours. Maybe less."

"There's got to be a way of taking care of him," I said. "I just haven't found it yet."

"You're not going to, either," she said bitterly. "I expected to fight him this time, but Baldy and Red left me. I thought I was paying them enough to hold them, but I guess there isn't enough money in the world to pay a man to face what looks like a sure bet to get killed."

I figured you could never buy loyalty from men like that, so I wasn't surprised they'd left, but I didn't say so. I asked: "What about this man Shell?"

She shrugged. "He belongs to Wallace, though I've got no proof of that."

Tug said softly: "He's here."

I turned to see Wallace stride around the corner of the big tent. He said: "I didn't expect to see you here, Sheriff. I thought you'd be hiding somewhere or getting on your horse and sloping out of town."

He'd probably seen me come here and had followed to put more pressure on me. I said: "I was aiming to hide, Wallace, but I haven't decided on what would be the safest place."

"Captain Wallace," he said angrily. "Damn it, I've told you often enough." He turned to Maggie. "Well, we seem to have run into each other again."

"How much?" she asked resignedly.

"I'm here to enforce the law," he said. "Somebody has to pay me. Your share is ten dollars a week, starting now."

"I'll get it," she said, and disappeared into the tent.

I wheeled and walked away. Tug hesitated, then caught up with me. "We can't do it, Mark," he said. "We just can't walk off and leave that bastard free to skim the cream off the top of this camp. It makes us both look like cowards."

Wallace wanted me out of the way and he wanted it now or he wouldn't have tried again so soon to make me mad enough to draw against him. It was an old game that doubtless had worked many times for him in the past and had paved the way for him to kill more men than he was likely to remember. Nobody wanted to be called a coward, and it rankled in me just as much as it did in Tug, but to give way to the rage that was building in me would be to hand the town over to Wallace.

"We'll move when the time is right, Tug," I said. "Not before." I looked at him and saw the overpowering anger that was ruling him. "You've got a wife and baby. Don't you forget it."

"I ain't forgetting," he said savagely. "I ain't forgetting that you're the boss, neither."

That hurt. He was saying what others were saying or would be saying—that Wallace was right about me being a coward. I said curtly: "You stay in the office tonight. Leave Wallace alone."

I wheeled away and strode toward my house. For the first time I wasn't sure I could hold off.

CHAPTER TWENTY-TWO

Abbie had supper on the stove when I reached the house. She gave me a searching look when I stepped into the kitchen, but when I didn't say anything, she said: "Supper will be ready in a few minutes."

I sat down at the table and smoked my pipe. Presently she brought the food to the table and took a chair across from me. We ate, still saying nothing, then she rose, picked up the dishes, and washed and dried them.

When she finished, she said: "I'm going home, Mark."

"I'll go with you," I said.

We walked through the twilight, my arm around her. When we reached her place, she said passionately: "It's mighty queer the way duty controls a man. You and I could leave here tonight and never come back. We could get married and have children and live a long and normal life together. Nobody in this town deserves anything from you."

Her face turned up to mine. I looked at it in the thin light and thought about saying that there would always be situations like this and a man couldn't run from them or he'd be running all of his life. I knew that was true, and I had certainly given a lot of thought to running.

I didn't say any of those things. Instead, I asked: "Is that what you want me to do?"

She took a long breath. "No, Mark," she whispered. "I guess it isn't."

"It'll be over soon," I said. "It's got to be."

I held her in my arms and kissed her. When I let her go, she whirled away from me and ran up the path to her front door. I watched her until she disappeared into the house, then I walked back through the twilight that was almost night now.

I didn't know what to do except to wait and that wasn't going to be easy. I didn't think I could sleep, and I wanted to be home when Garnet Wallace came, though I still had a feeling that it could be some kind of a trap that would give Wallace a chance to get at me. Still, I had to take that chance.

I was convinced that Mrs. Wallace was not a happy woman. Maybe, just maybe, she had something to tell me that would open a door for me. So far I hadn't hooked on to anything, so I couldn't afford to overlook a possibility.

I sat for a long time on my front porch, thinking I should be on Main Street, but I also thought that this situation was about to come to a head. I just had to give it time.

Wallace had said I had forty-eight hours. I suppose he thought I would panic in that time and leave town, or I would be driven into facing him. Sooner or later that's what I would have to do, but I wanted it on my terms and at a time of my choosing.

Midnight was slow coming. I got so jumpy I couldn't sit still, so I walked to the jail thinking I'd talk to Tug. The office was empty. I had told Tug to stay there, but he was nowhere in sight. That worried me, but I had no intention of hunting for him. If he wasn't going to play this my way, he'd have to take what came to him.

I did go on to Main Street and I stood on the corner for a time, watching the scene that had become familiar to me. The usual Saturday night crowd was on the street. The men were moving from one saloon to another, some drunk, some sober. Men stopped to talk; others pushed their way through or around the talkers so that there seemed to be a sort of pulsating movement in the flow of the crowd.

A fight would break out, usually between two men too drunk to hurt each other. Now and then a gun would go off, most of them aimed at the sky. The business district ran for several blocks now, and lamps in the saloons and gambling places and the flaming torches in front of the buildings made Main Street almost as bright as day. Laughter and angry shouts mingled together to make a strange, discordant sound.

On any other night I would have been in that crowd, trying to keep it moving, arresting drunks and stopping fights, and doing anything else I needed to do to keep order, but I had resolved that tonight I would stay out of it.

I wanted to see what Wallace would do. I did not see him, but I suppose that his mere presence in town intimidated the real troublemakers. In any case, nothing was happening that seemed out of order, so I turned back to my house.

I sat down again on my front porch. I didn't look at my watch, but I knew it was close to midnight. Presently I caught a hint of movement in front of the house. I rose and, drawing my gun, stood with my back to the wall.

I called: "Who's there?"

I half expected a bullet, to see the blossom of gunfire and hear the hammering explosion of a shot, but instead I heard a woman's voice: "It's Garnet Wallace." She ran up the path. When she reached the porch, she asked: "Where are you?"

"Here," I said, and put out a hand to her, still not sure she wouldn't greet me with a bullet, though I didn't think that would be Wallace's way. He would do his own killing in front of the entire town. He would lose the effect he sought if he didn't. Besides, I was convinced he enjoyed the act of killing another man.

She felt my hand on her arm and gripped it quickly. "Inside," she said softly. "I know I wasn't followed, but I don't like to take chances."

I led her through the door into the front room. "Shut and lock it," she said. I did, then she added: "Take me to your bedroom."

That made me nervous and I began to suspect some version of the old badger game. I said: "I don't want. . . ."

"I'm the one who's taking chances," she said sharply. "John will kill me if he finds out what I'm doing. Now do what I tell you."

I led her across the living room into the bedroom.

She said: "Shut the door and pull the blinds, then light a lamp."

I hesitated, but, having gone this far, I decided I'd be stupid not to see it through. As soon as I held a match to the wick and replaced the chimney, she said: "Good. Now get the blind down." I obeyed, then she said: "Watch carefully. I've got something to show you."

I smelled her perfume; I was very much aware of her sensuous body, and I had a strange feeling of being tugged in one direction and then the other.

She faced me and began to unbutton her blouse. I guess I stopped breathing because I knew what she was going to do. All of a sudden I could see Wallace smashing down my door and finding a scene that would give him every right to shoot me, thus putting the community behind what he did.

"Hold on!" I shouted. "I don't want . . . !"

"Oh, shut up," she said tartly. "I can find plenty of men to seduce without coming here. I've got something to show you." I guess she thought she hadn't convinced me yet, so she added: "I can find better-looking men than you to go to bed with."

That took the wind out of my sails. I couldn't dispute her last statement, so I stood there, motionless, my mouth open and I suppose my eyes bugged out of my head. Anyhow, she stood naked in front of me a moment later, and I had to admit that she had a beautiful and exciting body. I wanted her. Any man who looked at her would want her. I took a step toward her, but she held up a hand.

"No, damn it," she said. "Look, but don't touch. I told you I didn't come here to get into bed with you. You just take a good look at me. I'm a beautiful piece of female flesh. I attract men. I knew that because it used to be my business. I'm not John's wife. I'm a whore. He picked me out of a house in Bismarck three years ago. I belong to him, he says, therefore he can do anything to me he wants to.

"I was glad to go with him at first because I'd have done anything to get out of the damned whorehouse, but now I'll do anything to get back into one. He's a monster, Mister Girard, an animal. I want you to free me. I'll never be free as long as he's alive. I'm doing this to show you why I want him killed, and then I think you'll believe what I'm going to tell you."

She turned around slowly. I gasped and I guess I stopped breathing again for a moment. Her front side was beautiful and attractive; her back side was ugly and repulsive because it was a mass of scars and welts. Two of them were fresh, open and bloody wounds that must have been painful. I guessed they had been given to her within the last day or two.

She turned back to face me, asking: "Convinced?"

I nodded, and she began to dress. "I told you that you had put him into an ugly mood in Durango. When that happens, he always takes it out on me. That's why he whipped me. He calls you a cowboy sheriff and acts like he has nothing but contempt for you, but actually he's afraid of you."

"That's hard to believe," I said.

She shook her head. "No. You see, you haven't caved in. He's told me many times that men like you are the dangerous ones in the long run. He's determined to kill you, Mister Girard, but there's one thing you don't know and it's the last thing he wants you to know."

She didn't say anything more until she slipped on her blouse. By this time my brain was churning and I was willing to accept anything she told me. Maybe modesty had never been one of her virtues. Still, it had required courage to do what she had just done.

"Nobody would blame you if you killed him," I said.

In Durango I had thought that she was a smiling woman, as happy as any woman would be who had to live the way she did, moving from one town to another to be with her husband. Now there was no hint of a smile on her face, no indication that she was or ever had been a happy woman.

"I would kill him if I could," she said. "I tried once and failed, and he almost beat me to death. I guess I'm afraid to try again."

I nodded, understanding that. I asked: "You know something that would give me a chance against him?"

She hesitated as she finished buttoning her blouse. Finally she said: "Yes. I don't know what you can do or how you'll manage, but there is one thing I can tell you. Remember the man he killed this afternoon? You saw it?"

"Yes, I saw it," I answered.

"He shot the man from close range," she said. "That's the only way he can. His eyes are bad, so bad that at a distance everything is blurred. He has glasses, but he won't wear them. He doesn't want people to know."

Suddenly she began to cry. She whirled away from me and ran out of the room and on out of the house. I stood there, thinking about her, the scent of her perfume lingering in the air. I wondered if she had ever loved John Wallace, and whether she still loved him.

Again the thought came to me that maybe this was a trap. No, I didn't think so, not after seeing her back. I believed she felt she had delivered John Wallace into my hands, but, in spite of his abuse, she still had some love for him.

CHAPTER TWENTY-THREE

After Garnet Wallace left, I went to bed. I didn't think I could sleep, and I didn't. I simply lay there, staring into the darkness and thinking about John Wallace. Near dawn I got up, knowing I could not stand the bed another minute.

I built a fire and set the coffee pot and the teakettle on the stove. As soon as the water was hot, I shaved and for some reason that made no logical sense I put on a clean shirt. I drank a cup of coffee, buckled my gun around me, and left the house.

The sun wasn't up yet, but the opalescent light of dawn had brightened the eastern sky. I heard a dog bark from somewhere to the north, then a rooster crowed. The usual sounds of town life were muted at this hour except for the crack of axe on wood from the rear of the hotel. Joe Steele's handy man, Dombey, was cutting the day's supply of stove wood.

I paused, seeing that someone was running toward me. I gripped the butt of my gun. I didn't think it would be Wallace, but I was too jumpy to take any chances.

A moment later I saw that it was Dutch Henry. I asked: "What brings you out of bed before sunup?"

He gripped my arm, panting. For a moment he was unable to speak, then he managed: "By hokey, I shouldn't run. I'm too old." He swallowed and labored for breath, then said: "There's an old Dutch proverb that says it's always the darkest before the dawn."

Usually I was patient with his philosophizing, but not this

morning. I knew he had something important to tell me or he wouldn't have got out of bed before sunup. I demanded: "What's on your mind?"

"Two things," he said. "Last night Shell beat up Jerry Carruthers because he refused to pay a nickel for Wallace's salary."

"Did he say it that way?" I asked.

"Hell, no," Henry said. "It was the same old business about paying for protection against broken windows and fire and the like. He never mentioned Wallace's name."

"I didn't think he would," I said. "Wallace is too smart for that."

"Well, Tug was cruising around and he heard about it," Henry went on, "so he tried to arrest Shell, but Shell got to him with his fists and beat hell out of him. Him and Carruthers are both in Doc Jenner's place."

So that was why Tug had not been in the office last night. I asked: "Bad?"

"Bad enough," he answered. "They'll live and I reckon they won't be crippled, but they sure ain't gonna be doing much for a while." He took a long breath. "Now there's another thing. I didn't know if you was going after Shell or not, but, if you are, you'll find him asleep in the mow of our stable."

It took me a moment to digest that because I hadn't expected it. I said: "Yeah, I'm going after him."

"Don't let him get his hands on you," Henry warned. "That's where Tug made his mistake. He's a monster, Mark. By God, he must be part grizzly as big as he is."

"He'll never get his hands on me," I said. "I'll kill him if he tries."

I'd never killed a man in my life. As a matter of fact, I had only shot at a man once, at Ten-Sleep Morgan, and then not to kill. But I was prepared to kill now, and then I was going to shoot at Wallace, and yet in the back of my mind was the

knowledge that telling myself I was going to kill a man and doing it were two very different things.

As I strode toward the stable, I was very much aware of this,
but at the same time I knew I wouldn't let this giant tear me up
the way he had Tug Ralston. An officer wasn't supposed to
shoot an unarmed man, but Shell's hands were lethal weapons
and I wasn't going to forget it.

I went into the stable through the archway. It was quite dark
inside, although a lantern hung from a nail beside the office
door. I paused, letting my eyes become accustomed to the near
darkness, then I called: "Shell! Come down. You're under arrest. This is Sheriff Girard speaking."

No answer. I moved forward, my gun in my hand, and fired a
shot upward through the opening in front of the ladder that led
into the mow. I said: "Shell, I don't know where you are up
there, but if you don't come down, I'm going to scatter some
lead all over that haymow. The chances are good you'll get hit."

"What's the charge?" he asked, his voice the low rumble I'd
expect from a man of his size.

"Assault and battery," I answered, "and resisting an officer of
the law."

"I didn't resist Captain Wallace," he said sullenly, "and
Captain Wallace is the only officer of the law there is in this
two-bit town."

"You're wrong about that," I said. "I'm the sheriff and Tug
Ralston's a deputy. Now I don't want to have to kill you, but, if
you don't come down, that's just what I'm going to do."

"All right," he said, "and Captain Wallace will kill you for
what you're doing. Have you thought about that?"

"I've thought," I said, "which same won't do you any good.
Now I'm done palavering. Come on down."

"I'm coming," he said in a surly tone. "I'm coming, and
maybe I'll just work you over till your own mother wouldn't

recognize your ugly mug."

I saw his boots on the top rung of the ladder, then the rest of his huge body as he eased down one rung at a time. When he finally stood upright on the stable floor, I believed everything I had heard about him being a monster.

He must have stood at least six feet six inches, and I judged he'd weigh close to three hundred pounds. No fat, either. He was just damned big. I would have compared him to a gorilla instead of a grizzly. In fact, his rough features, hairy face, and long arms, and the way he stood with his shoulders hunched forward reminded me of a gorilla.

Shell started toward me, his huge fists swinging at his sides. As I backed up toward the archway, I said: "If you rush me, I'll kill you. I have no intentions of taking the beating my deputy took."

He laughed at me. His meaty lips sprang apart, then tightened. "You won't kill me, Sheriff. Nobody shoots an unarmed man. I don't reckon you will."

I kept backing up so that I maintained about the same distance between us. I sensed he was going to keep coming, that he didn't believe I would shoot. This had probably been the secret of his success. I had a hunch that Tug, who had his share of guts and would probably have tackled John Wallace himself if he'd had the opportunity, had not been able to pull the trigger on Shell when the big man had charged him.

Then Shell made up his mind and came at me in a rush, his head down. I lowered the muzzle of my gun enough to get him in the right leg instead of his guts and fired. I stepped back into the street because his momentum carried him another ten feet. When he went down, it was like falling a giant pine tree. He let out a yip of pain as he rolled over on his back, clutching his knee.

"You shot me," he said as if he still didn't believe it was possible. "Get the doc. Damn it, get the doc."

"Did you get the doc for Carruthers and Tug Ralston?" I asked.

"No, but. . . ."

"Then you can crawl to the doc's office," I said. "As soon as you're able to travel, you get out of this camp and stay out."

"Captain Wallace will kill you for this, you son-of-a-bitch!" he bellowed. "He'll kill you."

I still had no absolute evidence that Shell was Wallace's man, but I thought this was enough. I headed for the hotel, knowing now what I was going to do, and knowing, too, that I could put it off no longer. Regardless of how the fight with Wallace came out, I felt better just knowing what I was going to do.

CHAPTER TWENTY-FOUR

No one was at the desk in the hotel. The night man had gone and Joe Steele was not up yet. At this hour no one was around and Steele was tardy getting to the desk. A bachelor, he slept in a room back of the lobby and took his meals in the hotel dining room.

I had reached the point where I couldn't risk delay, so I circled the desk and opened the door of Steele's room. He lay on his back, snoring, his mouth open. I shook him awake, but he must have been up late because he was far down and it was a full minute before he got his eyes open enough to know who I was.

"What the hell's the matter with you, Mark?" he muttered, rubbing his eyes. "I just got to bed. That damned Wallace worked up a poker game and wouldn't quit. He didn't go to bed until two o'clock. He took me for fifty dollars."

"Get up," I said. "Put on your clothes."

"Now you just wait a dog-gone minute," Steele said angrily. "I've got a right to sleep in my own bed as long as I want to. This is pretty high-handed for you to come in here and. . . ."

"Get your clothes on, Joe," I said. "I've got a job for you."

He rubbed his eyes again and took another look at me, then started to dress. I don't know whether there was something in my face or in the tone of my voice, but he stopped arguing. He pulled his pants on and stood up.

"All right," he said sullenly. "What is it?"

"You're going to Wallace's room and wake him up," I said, "and. . . ."

"Oh no, I ain't doing any such thing," he exploded. "I told you he didn't go to bed until two o'clock this morning. He aims to sleep till noon. That son-of-a-bitch would shoot me if I woke him up now."

"If you don't do what I tell you," I said, "I'll shoot you. Now take your choice."

He took another long look at me and asked: "What's got into you, Mark? You've turned into a wild man."

"I reckon so," I said. "You and Rip and the others brought Wallace here and now it's up to me to get rid of him. I'm going to kill him, Joe. I never have killed a man, but I can kill a mad dog, and that's what Wallace is. You know it as well as I do. I just shot his man, Shell. Now are you going to wake him up?"

"You can't fight it out with Wallace," Steele said. "We never aimed for it to come to this. We'll get along with him somehow. He'll bleed us white just like you said, but that's better than having you killed."

"He's not going to kill me," I said. "You wake him up. Tell him I'm coming to arrest him. If he wants a chance at me, tell him to be in the street in ten minutes. He's anxious to get me out of the way, so he won't turn this chance down."

Steele rubbed his face. "It's a bad dream," he said. "No, by God, it's a nightmare."

"Tell him," I said. "I'm running out of patience." I looked at my watch. "Ten minutes. Get him into the street if you don't want your hotel shot up and maybe some of your customers killed."

I turned and stomped out of the hotel. He would do it, I thought, and Wallace would accept my challenge. He would assume that I'd wait until he made his draw, that it would be the traditional street duel with both of us pacing toward each other until we were fifteen or twenty feet apart, and then I'd allow him the first move. Well, that was where Captain John Wallace was going to get fooled.

As far as I was concerned, the old traditions that Wallace had lived by for so long didn't apply any more. I had not given up my authority and I had no intention of doing so. If he would not submit to arrest, and I knew he wouldn't, then I would kill him—if I could.

The strange part of it was that at that moment I was not afraid. It had been only a few minutes before that I had decided how I could make my move. I had to do this before I lost my courage, and I would if I waited.

I strode rapidly to my office and took a revolver off the gun rack. I saw that it was loaded. I checked the action and slipped it under my waistband on the left side. Then I checked the gun in my holster and eased it back into leather.

I left the office. When I reached the front of the livery stable, the sun was barely showing above the eastern ridges. I would be facing it, but for a few minutes it would not be high enough to bother my vision.

It was then ten minutes from the time I had left the hotel. I waited, alone in the street. I had a strange sensation about that. In another hour or so wagons and men on foot and on horseback would choke the street, but now I saw no one.

I glanced at my watch. Ten minutes, but no Wallace. Another minute. Still no Wallace. I began having doubts. If I had to go into the hotel after him, the odds would be against me. I had bet my life on the assumption that he could not turn down a challenge, but now I began to wonder.

Twelve minutes! I could not wait much longer. I had to go after him. I had made my proposition to Joe Steele. If Wallace didn't show in the street, I'd have to make my threat good. Then I saw him leave the hotel and step into the street, and I felt the quick relaxing that comes from release of tension. I could do it, I told myself. I had to.

"You're under arrest, Wallace!" I called. "Drop your gun belt."

"Captain Wallace, damn it," he yelled angrily. "Now what trumped-up charge are you arresting me for?"

"Fraud," I shouted back. "Hiring a man to commit assault. Conspiracy to extort money from the business people of Angel's Landing. That'll do for a start. Now drop your gun belt and put your hands up or I'll start shooting. If you resist arrest, I'll kill you."

At this distance and in the thin morning light I could not see whether his usually expressionless face was still expressionless, but I could imagine what this man, who had done more killing than he could remember, must be feeling about being arrested by a man he had called a cowboy sheriff. Maybe he was stirred by the exhilaration that likely came to him before each kill. I had no way to know.

He didn't drop his gun belt, but of course I had known he wouldn't. He started toward me, slowly, deliberately, his right hand swinging at his side but never more than a few inches from the butt of his gun.

"I'll give you five seconds," I said. "Either drop your gun belt or make your play."

"I'll make my play when I'm close enough for accurate shooting," he snarled.

I waited the five seconds, and then I drew my gun and began to shoot. We were much too far apart. I saw that my first bullet kicked up dust in front of him, the second slightly to his right, and then it happened as I had hoped it would. He panicked. He yelled something derogatory about my ancestry and drew his gun and started running toward me.

My third bullet was close, close enough to clip the crown of his hat. He yelled an oath and began shooting, but if Garnet had told me the truth, and I was gambling my life that she had, he was still too far away to see me clearly. He fired three times, each shot short, but he was close enough to make me uncomfortable.

I took my time with my fourth shot. I got him in the chest, knocking him partly around. He fired again, his slug ripping open a shallow wound along my right side, then my fifth shot knocked him down.

I jammed my gun back into leather and drew the second with my left hand and transferred it to my right. I paced slowly toward him, the morning sun now quite bright, in front of me, my long shadow trailing me. The echoes of the last shot died. I kept moving, watching his right hand.

He had dropped his gun, and now, lying on his belly with life flowing out of him, he tried to reach it. His fingertips dug into the street dust, but he could not find the strength to extend his fingers those last two inches which separated him from the butt of his .45.

"You bastard," he whispered. "You trapped me." A bloody froth ran from his mouth down his chin and on down his neck. "You knew, didn't you?"

At this moment of his death I could not tell him that the woman he had abused had given him away, so I said nothing. I stood there, looking down at him and watching him die. For some strange reason I felt apart from all of this, almost as if I had not done it, that I was someone else, a spectator who was watching this final scene. I felt no guilt, no remorse, only a great relief that this man who had indeed been a madman was no longer a threat to me or anyone in Angel's Landing.

Slowly men came into the street, Yager from his saloon and Joe Steele from the hotel and Doc Jenner from his office. Others were there, too, some I knew and some I didn't. Doc Jenner turned the body over. There were two bullet holes in his chest, but one slug had hit Wallace's big star and been partly deflected by it. Then, and the fact startled me, I saw that his star, twisted and bent out of shape by my bullet, now was smaller than mine.

I looked up at the second story of the hotel and saw Garnet's face pressed against a window. She was free, I thought. John Wallace would never beat her again.

Yager came to me, moving slowly, a shaky old man. He said, his voice trembling: "We'll see that you get the other two men that you need, Mark."

I turned away, sick of the whole business, and started to run toward Abbie's house. I wanted her to know that it was over.

ABOUT THE AUTHOR

Wayne D. Overholser won three Spur Award from the Western Writers of America and has a long list of fine Western titles to his credit. He was born in Pomeroy, Washington, and attended the University of Montana, University of Oregon, and the University of Southern California before becoming a public schoolteacher and principal in various Oregon communities. He began writing for Western pulp magazines in 1936 and within a couple of years was a regular contributor to Street & Smith's *Western Story Magazine* and Fiction House's *Lariat Story Magazine*. *Buckaroo's Code* (1947) was his first Western novel and remains one of his best. In the 1950s and 1960s, having retired from academic work to concentrate on writing, he would publish as many as four books a year under his own name or a pseudonym, most prominently as Joseph Wayne. *The Violent Land* (1954), *The Lone Deputy* (1957), *The Bitter Night* (1961), and *Riders of the Sundowns* (1997) are among the finest of the Overholser titles. *The Sweet and Bitter Land* (1950), *Bunch Grass* (1955), and *Land of Promises* (1962) are among the best Joseph Wayne titles, and *Law Man* (1953) is a most rewarding novel under the Lee Leighton pseudonym. Overholser's Western novels, whatever the byline, are based on a solid knowledge of the history and customs of the 19th-Century West, particularly when set in his two favorite Western states, Oregon and Colorado. Many of his novels are first-person narratives, a technique that tends to bring an added dimension of vividness to the frontier experiences of his narrators and frequently, as in *Cast a Long Shadow* (1957), the female characters one encounters are among the most memorable. He wrote his numerous novels with a consistent skill and an uncommon sensitivity to the depths of human character. Almost invariably, his stories weave a spell of their own with their scenes and images of social and economic forces often in conflict and the diverse ways of life and personalities that made the American Western frontier so unique a time and place in human history. *Beyond the Law* will be his next Five Star Western.